He on Honeydew Hath Fed

Tales of the City and Abroad

W. E. Smith

Also by W. E. Smith

Novels

Be True to Your Tribe (under the pen name Moose Eliot)
Tanaki on the Shore
Ver Sacrum, or Heaven Help Us All
Bal Harbour
I've Got a Right to Sing the Blues

Stories

I Wanna Hear It Again

Copyright © 2018 W. E. Smith
All rights reserved
ISBN: 13: 978-0-9984847-3-0
ISBN: 0-9984847-3-0

He on Honeydew Hath Fed

Tales of the City and Abroad

Table of Contents

Alladin's International Bookstore

There once lived a poor tailor, who had a son called Aladdin, a careless, idle boy who would do nothing but play all day long in the streets with little idle boys like himself . . .

IN THOSE DAYS he thought he knew some things because he was listening to João Gilberto and Bill Evans and reading the Latin historians. Three years out of college, he was still living at his mother's apartment: he and his mother and sister, the rump remains of a family fractured by his father's attachment to a secretary at his office; the discovery of the affair by his mother; the old man's pyschological breakdown; and the myriad upheavals which ensued. But what troubled Rick Baxter even more than all of this was the question of what he was supposed to do with the rest of his still-young life; something, he adduced, having to do with setting himself up on his own, meeting a good woman, and finding a world with no place in it for the kind of things that had happened to his family. The hateful prospect of returning to law school hovered menacingly over his consciousness, but more immediate was the day-to-day life he was enmeshed in, Dean and Nousha and the others at the shop, his friends Tom and Hector, Shirley, and then Dawn.

Had it not been for Dean and Nousha he would have

been lost. He had found Alladin's International Bookstore through the listing in the Yellow Pages. He was looking for a place to buy French novels, and Alladin's was closer than the downtown shop whose wooden shelves were packed with the distinctive bindings of European and South American publishing houses. The bell jangled when he pulled the glass door stamped with an image of the famous lamp and stepped out of the noisy glare of Rockville Pike, that ugly commercial drag that cleaves the suburbs north of the capital city. He moved into the quiet shop, aware of the muted green carpet, the tall metal bookshelves, and a sales counter behind which a squat Arab in a natty sports coat gazed on some paperwork.

"Welcome to Alladin's," the man said in a voice that, though forthright, seemed to bubble up through some viscous liquid, his words drowning in a sea of emotional depth Rick Baxter could not begin to sound. "Can I help you find something?"

"No thanks, I'm just looking," Rick replied, reluctant to disclose a mission so out of place among the mass-consumerism of what locals referred to simply as *the Pike*.

"Please, help yourself." The Arab's tone would have been deferential, had it not been for the impregnability of his stance, the easy but dense gravity of his physique.

Rick stepped slowly along the shelves and scanned the English as a Second Language series that made up the bulk of Alladin's inventory, their cheerful covers beckoning huddled masses to lives of granted wishes in the land of milk, honey, and MacDonald's. He had resigned himself to having wasted an hour on a fruitless errand when the Arab suddenly appeared between the shelves.

"Are you sure I can't help you find something?" he said. "We carry all the major publishers."

"I was actually looking for novels in French," Rick began hesitantly. "Perhaps I misread the Yellow Pages listing."

"Oh no, we have them. Please, right this way."

Rick followed the man to the front of the shop where, next to the sales counter, a metal rack carried a few dozen paperbacks. "Here they are," the man said, "feel free to take a look."

Greedily scanning the titles on the rack, Rick barely noticed the Arab return to his place behind the counter. Though the selection was limited, and many of the volumes jaundiced and tattered, he found a serviceable copy of *Père Goriot* and an annotated version of *Ruy Blas*. He approached the counter with his selections.

"Ah, I see you found what you were looking for," the Arab said with what struck Rick Baxter as a forced heartiness.

"Yes, thank you."

The man busied himself looking at price lists, turning the volumes one way and another, and then he scoured the inside covers. Apparently he didn't know what to charge for his own merchandise.

"Let's say two dollars for both."

"That's fine."

"By the way," the man continued, "I'm Dean, *Alla' din Al-Quraishi*, that is." He proffered a pudgy hand over the counter, and Rick took it gladly.

"Rick Baxter."

"You speak French?"

"I'm not fluent."

"I guess you work in the neighborhood."

"I'm not employed at the moment."

"Hmm," Dean Al-Quraishi said. "I need some-body to help around here. Would you be interested?" Rick glanced around the shop, weighing the prospect of spending his days there . . . and remembering that his small savings would soon run out.

"Can you type?"

"Sure."

"Why don't you come back Monday and meet my wife, Wendy."

&&&

"Good morning," Dean said cheerfully when Rick stepped into the shop on Monday morning.

"Good morning."

Dean looked on while Rick took notice of a woman standing on the customer side of the counter.

"Well," Dean said, "this is Wendy."

Rick fixed his eyes on the owlish woman, the aquiline nose, wide, all-seeing eyes, a quiet, unblinking calm. She stood a good six inches over her husband, her hips boxy, graying hair hanging limply from a central part, her com-plexion blotchy. She wore a formless denim skirt that cov-ered her knees, a loose-fitting blouse, flat shoes, and had a hairy mole on one cheek that irritated Rick Baxter but did not seem to concern Wendy Al-Quraishi in the least. She faced Rick.

"Happy to meet you," she said in a voice as birdish as her appearance, musical in a softly modulated way. She held out a limp hand. Rick clasped it briefly.

"We thought Wendy could show you the system we use to track inventory. Right, Wendy?"

"Yes, that's right, Dean," she said in her measured tones.

"We just started the shop last year, so we're still getting organized. Wendy's the brains behind the operation."

Wendy blushed, and she hung her head in a way that required her to pull her hair from her eyes in order to look shyly up at Rick Baxter.

Rick spoke to counter the impression that his recruitment was a *fait accompli*. "What exactly do you have in mind my doing here?"

Dean exhaled forcefully, placed his stocky forearms, bare below the rolled-up sleeves of a blue Oxford shirt, on the counter, and leaned toward his wife. "Wendy?"

"We need some help keeping track of the stock," Wendy said, "and to help with customers, especially when Dean and I aren't here."

With that she fell silent and stood looking at the floor.

"Wendy," Dean put in after a respectful pause, "aren't you forgetting about the catalogue?"

Wendy pulled her hair out of her eyes and smiled sweetly at her husband. "Why don't you tell him about that, dear," she demurred. "The catalogue is your idea."

"Wendy doesn't like the marketing part," Dean said with a chuckle. "But you know what they say in business, advertise or die!"

Wendy blushed again.

"You see," Dean continued, "Wendy and I started the business because there wasn't any place where ESL teachers could see all the instructional series under one roof."

"It was a pain choosing materials," Wendy added with

considerable feeling, but no bitterness.

"Wendy was a teacher, and I had the business know-how. So we put our heads together and came up with this place."

Dean looked approvingly around the little store and then fell into a satisfied silence.

"Dean," Wendy reminded gently, "aren't you going to tell Rick about the catalogue?"

"Oh yes, of course," Dean said, raising himself from the counter, clasping his hands before his chest with an energetic relish. "The catalogue is my secret weapon, the final part of the plan. We have the store up and running, but we need to let people know we're here, and all the wonderful things we carry."

"I see."

"Once we have our catalogue, teachers won't need to go through all the different publishers' catalogues. All the ESL materials will be listed in one place—in our catalogue. Then, if they want to review anything, they can come in here and see it."

"Makes sense."

"Have you ever done anything like this before?" Dean asked.

Rick said that he had worked with a small press at the law school, a publisher of legal manuals.

"Rick, something tells me you're just the guy I'm looking for. When can you start?"

Rick Baxter glanced at Wendy and then back to Dean. They seemed helpless, a neediness that attracted him, in spite of his determined self-centeredness. There was also the matter of his rapidly diminishing savings. He squeezed Dean's hand firmly.

"Anytime."

&&&

Over the days and weeks that followed, Rick became part of Alladin's International Bookstore. Wendy acquainted him with the index cards on which she had recorded, in a careful hand, each title carried by the enterprise, along with the publisher and date of publication, number of pages, price, and a line or two of description. Dean showed him how to receive shipments from publishers and prepare orders—sometimes quite large ones—for shipment to institutional customers. For reasons mysterious to Rick, the owner quickly developed a blind faith in his abilities as well as his trustworthines; he soon had him fielding phone inquiries and handling the sales floor.

But Dean's most cherished project remained the catalogue, and after Rick's general orientation, his time was increasingly spent in a cubbyhole at the rear of the shop before a big brown electric typewriter. There he sat, surrounded by Wendy's index cards and handsomely done publishers' catalogues, cribbing enthusiastic blurbs from the publishers' fulsome descriptions, doing his best to avoid outright plagiarism.

He soon made the acquaintance of Dean's other employees. There was Shadi, short and compactly built, with dark, lively eyes, a pert little mouth, and tightly curled hair. She was a student at the community college, and appeared at the shop, like all of Dean's employees save Rick, at irregular intervals. She was Persian, as was Nousha, with whom Rick developed a thriving friendship until one day he simply never saw her again. Nousha was married to a gentle, tolerant, and bespectacled man Rick never got to know but occasionally chatted with when he picked up Nousha from work. They were childless, and as far as Rick could tell, Nousha had few obligations beyond taking care of her husband and the occasional hours at the shop. She and Rick hit it off when they discovered a mutual interest in French literature, a broad spiritual ethics, and all things transcendent and poetic. Esfir, another Persian, came in on occasion. She was at once more elegant, more worldly, and more practical-minded then Nousha; but then Nousha was, as far as Rick could tell, a saint. Besides this trio, there was a brilliant high school student, a lanky blond kid devoted to mastering Scriabin's piano literature, physics, and several foreign languages (at the time Rick met him, he was intent on tackling Sanskrit, so that he could read the *Bhagavad Gita* in the original). When he came into the shop after school, a day or two every week, he and Rick discussed the probability of the big bang theory, the existence of God, strategic decisions of Roman generals during the Punic Wars, and the relative difficulties of learning Italian and Spanish.

& & &

Rick continued to read the ancient historians and French novels, listen to jazz records, and occasionally meet his friends Tom and Hector downtown to take in a foreign film at the art cinema. Everything Rick did in those days was calculated to make him different, as different as possible from the All-American father who had broken his family's heart.

Across the landing from his mother's place, Shirley beckoned with a standing offer to share her bed. Rick would bury his face in her hair as it lay splayed across the sheets, breathing in patchouli and musk, being careful not to wake her son in the next room.

Shirley would come over to his mother's place. She would visit with Rick and his mother and sister, and if the kid wasn't with her there was a solid chance she would eventually say to Mrs. Baxter, after they all sat around listening to Rick beat out old chestnuts on the piano, "Well, Mrs. Baxter, do you mind if I borrow your son for a while?" Then, on the pretext of some manly chore she needed help with, she'd take him across the hall and jump him. Although he didn't believe for a minute that Shirley was the one he was looking for, Rick allowed this state of affairs to continue because it was easy and he didn't mind the sex; because Shirley seemed to understand, if not prefer, that he was not making any commitments; and because he liked and, yes, probably even needed her in some friendly kind of way. Both of them were saturated with the same hippy sensibilities. They enjoyed listening to music together, discussing New Agey conceptions of freedom and health, and decrying the politics of the Reagan administration. She often reeked of the hospital where she worked as a nurse, a mixture of disinfectant, medicines, death, and fear, but this was mostly compensated by her easygoing and tolerant nature.

&&&

Rick is standing near the counter at the front of the shop with Dean, a place made bright by plate glass windows that run across the length of the storefront.

"Tell me Rick, why did you quit law school?" Dean asks. "A guy with your brains! I'll bet you could go to the top."

Rick has gotten used to Dean's flattery, which he wants to imagine is at least partly sincere.

"It wasn't challenging enough," Rick says as he fusses with a mock-up for the catalogue. "It got boring."

"Now Rick, I know you're smart. But law school, not challenging?"

"Sure," Rick says, "you have to go through umpteen gyrations to come up with the correct answer. But there's no creativity. Law school just teaches you to think like everyone else."

"Is there something wrong with that?" Dean glances over at Rick's work.

"Look where it's gotten us." Rick turns the mock-up this way and that, pondering it.

"What do you mean?"

"What I mean is that this society is a mess."

"Believe me, it could be a lot worse."

"Perhaps," Rick concedes. "Maybe I'm looking for a greater sense of adventure in life." He makes another adjustment to the mock-up and stares intently upon it.

"Rick, take it from me, adventure isn't everything it's cracked up to be. Right, Wendy?"

Wendy is looking through a carton of books, paying the men no mind. "What?" she says dreamily, pulling hair from her eyes as she looks up.

"I was saying to Rick that adventure isn't everything it's cracked up to be."

"Well, I guess that's true."

"Wendy knows some of the adventures I've been

through," Dean takes up again. "Try living in Saddam Hussein's Iraq. There's an adventure for you! Or seeing your father hauled away by a bunch of goons, just for publishing an article. Those adventures I could have done without, believe me."

Dean Al-Quraishi's father was an economics professor at Baghdad's most prestigious university, Rick learned over time, until he was imprisoned for writing an article critical of the country's dictatorial Baath regime.

Wendy goes back to her books while Dean shuffles absently through the mail.

"I suppose it's also the insanity of the adversarial system," Rick says, finally fixing the mock-up at one angle, satisfied with his deliberations.

"What?"

"You know, everyone bent on getting their own way. In law, that means discounting anything running to your adversary's favor. I'm uncomfortable with people squaring off as enemies. They take it all so seriously, their petty rights and prerogatives."

"At least we have some rights here," Dean says. "Believe me, you should be grateful for that."

&&&

Rick is in his cubbyhole. He sits at a masonite table on which rests the big electric typewriter. A partition separates his "office" from the display floor in front. Attached to the partition, above the table, a couple of shelves carry dictionaries, catalogues, paper reams, and assorted office supplies. More publishers' catalogues are scattered across the table. A dark cotton curtain, as in some Baghdad bazaar, hangs across the entrance to the space, and across from this makeshift doorway is the bathroom. From time to time there is the sound of the toilet flushing, a door opens, and the aromas of human waste and artificial air freshener waft into his lair.

Nousha pulls back the edge of the curtain and peeks in. Rick is delighted to see her there.

"Rick," she says in her highly inflected Persian accent, "how are you?"

"Not bad."

"Can I come in?"

"Of course."

As usual, she seems a little giddy, an emotional all dressed up and no place to go. Hers is a lively spirit, eyes full of curiosity, but also an indiscriminate compassion. She sits down.

"I'm supposed to be taking inventory," she says with a conspiratorial smile, assuming Rick's consensus that no sentient being would take seriously the tedious chores which constitute her work at the shop.

"Is Dean still here?"

"He went next door." She pulls a heavy mass of long, thick hair behind one shoulder.

"Rick," she begins with a note of breathless concern in her voice, "I've been reading that novel you loaned to me."

"The Cortázar?"

"Yes, that one. *Hopscotch*."

"How do you like it?"

"She presses her broad lips together, battling her ingrained courtesy to release an unpleasant truth she cannot contain. Her face again relaxes, and then she says, with a certain rapture, "It's very poetic."

"Yes, I agree."

"You know I love Paris too much."

"*So* much."

"Right." She laughs at her habitual malapropism. "So much."

Peering across the level of the table, her expression grows serious. "Rick, do you think that Cortázar believes in God?"

"I can't really say, but judging from his writings, I doubt it."

"Oh," she says, nodding slowly. "Do you think that he's an existentialist?"

"Perhaps. Maybe he's more of a sybarite. Do you know what I mean?"

"Sybareet?" she pronounces in French.

"Yes, that's it. But there's also his political activism. You'd have to read *Manual for Manuel*. Frankly, I don't know how to label him. He's probably written about it somewhere."

"I didn't like the part too much about the baby," she says suddenly.

"What, where the baby dies?"

"Mmm," she nods in affirmation; she is obviously troubled.

Rick has never dwelt on this episode from *Hopscotch*, where the infant child of La Maga, Horacio Oliveira's lover, dies while Horacio and his friends, showing little concern, carry on with a party in the next room.

"They didn't seem to care about the baby."

"Why, because Horacio won't interrupt the party to tell

La Maga that the child had died?"

"Yes," she says soberly, her face locked in concentration, "but also because he didn't like that she had the baby to begin with. He seems so . . . how do you say . . . with no heart?" Her expression goes neutral. Rick understands that this is her way of retreating enough, having made a contrary remark, to allow her interlocutor to respond without uneasiness.

Still Rick is discomfited. Cortázar is one of his gods; and Oliveira, the protagonist of the Argentine's great masterwork—and the "pseudo-student" existence he leads in 1950's Paris, along with a group of Bohemian friends he calls "the Club"—represent for Rick a world of intellectual, social, and creative freedom that stands in stark, even desperate, contrast to the bitterly shrunken options offered along "the Pike." Seduced by Cortázar's expressive virtuosity, brilliantly evident in Rabassa's masterful English translation, as well as his fluent erudition and depth of honesty, it has never occurred to Rick to find fault with any aspect of the great writer's work; or for that matter, with his protagonist Oliveira, who in Rick's mind is thoroughly identified with Cortázar himself. He can only respond to Nousha's remarks by saying, "He might indeed be heartless, if you want to put it that way."

Then, because he doesn't like the tone of disagreement that has crept into their discussion, Rick pulls from beneath a publisher's catalogue a sheet of paper on which are scribed, in dark pencil, row upon row of Arabic characters.

"Oooh," Nousha intones with open joy, "let me see." She looks over the paper carefully. "They're good," she says with satisfaction, "really . . . beautiful."

Nousha has begun to teach Rick the Arabic alphabet, along with some simple Farsi expressions.

"Let me just show you . . ."

She takes up a pencil and begins to correct Rick's mistakes, patiently explaining each error. They are still absorbed in this procedure when Dean pokes his head past the curtain; they hadn't noticed the front bell jangling.

"Okay you guys," he says flatly, "no more goofing off. Let's get back to work."

"Sorry, Dean." Nousha gets up, glancing at Rick with a knowing smile. Meanwhile Rick distracts Dean with a discussion of the catalogue, showing him the progress he has made. This captures Dean's imagination.

"So when do you think we'll be finished?" he asks expectantly.

"Who knows," Rick replies, gesturing at the piles of publishers' catalogues that surround him.

"I hope it's not too long. We really need to get moving on the marketing."

This kind of talk makes little impact on Rick. Like Wendy, the business part doesn't much interest him. But he feels Dean's impatience, and he would like to see him content.

"I'll redouble my efforts."

"But Rick," Dean intones seriously, "can you re-triple them?"

The front bell jangles, and Dean strides hopefully through the curtain toward the sales floor.

&&&

So life went on like this for Rick, in those years after he dropped out of law school with no plan for the future other than to find something that seemed true for him. He took out Shadi, the only one of the three Persian women who wasn't married, a couple of times, but the relationship never threatened to exceed the bounds of friendship. When a young Frenchwoman came to work at the shop Rick asked her out too, using his best French; and when she turned him down he told her that he was *desolé*—not because he was really desolated, but because it seemed the right thing to say when a French girl turns you down.

The French girl didn't last long, but she stayed long enough to tell Rick that he seemed more European than American (an opinion in which Nousha concurred) and this made Rick happy, because in those days he thought everything European must be far superior to things American. Then it was back to Dean and Wendy and the three Persians and the high school kid, and Rick was comfortable with them, and for a while life was almost okay. He only figured out much later that Alladin's International Bookstore was a haven for refugees: for Dean from the brutality of Hussein's regime; for Wendy from an America that was speeding ever more rapidly away from index cards, grammar and shapeless cotton dresses; for the Persians from the lunacy of rule by Ayatollahs; for the high school kid, from a life full of non-geniuses; and for Rick, from himself. When he looked back, many years later, he was struck by how this unlikely gathering coalesced day by day, Sunni and Shia, American and foreign, poetic and practical, older and younger. But their differences were not important—with the Iran-Iraq war raging, and hundreds of thousands dying on the front lines, Dean and the Persians worked and laughed like favorite cousins who had grown up together—and they had all found a place where, for the present at least, they could simply *be*.

It's hard to say where this might have led—whether they would have formed themselves into some new tribe and migrated together to the deep woods or some island, declared themselves a state, or asked for protection under the United Nations—had Nousha not introduced Rick to Dawn, which for Rick began the unraveling of everything that then rested in unsteady equilibrium in his life.

Rick had in any case been wanting to cool things down with Shirley. Though she was a fine friend, he didn't really like the patchouli, or her apparent lack of any aspiration beyond raising her kid and having sex on a waterbed, and he knew that things would never go anywhere. She had moved away from his mother's building, and though they still dated, there was no longer the too-easy temptation to walk across the landing; consequently, they saw increasingly less of one another.

Dawn was a young woman whom Nousha had gotten to know at the community college, and Nousha invited Rick to a party at her family's home so that he might meet her. There were more than a dozen people there, all Persian except for Rick and Dawn; and after a meal of Middle Eastern delicacies, they danced the way Rick had seen Anthony Quinn dance in *Zorba the Greek* at the repertory cinema; and Rick himself was even persuaded to join in, aided in his efforts by good, red Persian wine.

It should not have been surprising that Nousha's matchmaking was transparent, for she was the most guileless person Rick had ever known. She seated Rick beside Dawn at dinner and made every effort to bring them together. Dawn, though quiet, was attractive and polite. Rick was nervous and learned only that she was interested in painting and took classes at the community college. Nonetheless when the evening ended he asked if he could see her again, because Nousha seemed to have arranged things that way; and Rick intuited that he, like some kind of Telemachus, needed the guidance of a goddess if he were ever to find his rightful destiny.

It turned out that Dawn was bright. She also took an interest in things that Rick and Nousha found fascinating, like Pablo Neruda's poetry, French music of the Belle Époque era, art films, and the ideas of Carlos Castaneda. Dawn had little family of her own. Her mother lived alone on the other side of town; her father, who had abandoned them when she was a child, was somewhere in California. She stayed with a family for whom she worked as an au pair; Rick would visit her there when her employers went out on Friday nights. They were both questing for something: something like home, or some way to put together shattered fragments of what was once whole and beautiful—or at any rate should have been whole and beautiful.

The camaraderie Dawn provided inspired Rick to try to get to the bottom of his malaise. They traveled together bound for Mexico, where Rick hoped to shed the sadness of his family and write beautiful words. But Dawn was intimidated by the roughness of Nuevo Laredo and the surly menace of the men at the bus station, and this after Rick had said things that were insensitive and wrong. She decided instead on California.

Rick followed her there, but they quarreled and she moved north, trying to find her father. Rick stayed on for a few months, living in a rented room, piecing a bare living together with restaurant jobs. But nothing worked and everything soon caught up with him and he had what in his parents' day was called a nervous breakdown, but was now called panic attacks and anxiety and clinical depression . . .

He found himself back at his mother's apartment, and he was seeing a therapist once a week. He checked in at Alladin's Bookstore. Changes were going down there. Dean's business model had never been sound (the publishers who supplied the shop would not grant Alladin's discounts larger than those offered at retail) and the enterprise was not thriving. Dean and Wendy, having accepted the inevitable, were winding things down. They needed help, and Dean gave Rick some hours.

"You know," he said one day while Rick quietly packed books by the front door, "I think California made you flaky."

As crudely frank as was Dean's remark, Rick knew that there was caring, as well as truth, behind it. Rick's California adventure *had* changed him. He once thought he knew some things, but now he wasn't sure if he knew anything. He had made a huge stab at breaking free of everything that had spelled chagrin—living at his mother's, Rockville Pike, Shirley—and now was back where he had started. He was still having panic attacks, and he often failed to get out of bed in the morning. In place of the confident, can-do young man who had walked into Alladin's two years earlier looking for French novels, there appeared a humbled, tentative introvert. Shirley picked him up at the apartment one day and they went out for lunch. Rick was quiet and distant, and she also told him, while driving home, that he was a changed person.

His friends Hector and Tom dropped by on occasion, but he seldom met them downtown anymore. They must have noticed how different he seemed, but neither mentioned it. Having known him longer than the others, they no doubt figured that the real Rick was still in there somewhere, and would emerge with time.

One day Nousha came to the shop. She and Rick lunched at a pizza joint across the Pike where Dean used to take everyone when he was in a good mood, typically because some English teacher from the community college had placed an especially large order.

"You're different," she said, and she peered deeply into him. "Your eyes are so sad."

After that Rick didn't see Nousha much, and when he did, she seemed aloof. Looking back later, he suspected that she felt uncomfortable that she had brought him and Dawn together, and that things had gone badly for him.

But Rick was getting the help he needed, finally confronting the pyschic wounds engendered by his father's reckless behavior: the pain that Nousha saw in his eyes was not the pain of present trauma, but the pain of past trauma being healed. His intellectualism, his other-ness, had all been a gigantic shield with which to defend himself against the wound of his shattered family.

Without Dawn, Rick would have never faced these things. For their brief affair, disastrous as it was, gave him a taste of what might be possible if he were to let go of the past and seek his happiness in earnest.

There was much he still had to learn, but before long he found another job and moved out of his mother's place. He married a cellist, a decent sort, and began to find a little more of himself . . .

He never saw Dean again, but during the Gulf War, when newscasts featured nightly accounts of the persecution of Arab Americans, he looked him up in the phone book and gave him a call.

"Believe me, Rick," Dean assured him, "this is nothing compared to living under Hussein." He and Wendy seemed to be getting by, and after a brief chat, they said goodbye.

Rick never spoke to Dean again, nor did he ever again encounter the others from Alladin's Bookstore for Refugees from International Mayhem and Family Disorder.

But he would never, ever, forget them.

In those days he thought he knew some things, because he was listening to Bill Evans and João Gilberto and reading the Latin historians . . .

Circular Breathing

CIRCULAR BREATHING is an advanced technique. Even Bethann hadn't mastered it, and she was considered, by people who could judge such matters, one of the finest flutists of her generation. One might say of breath, even more so than in regard to other wind instruments, that it is the soul of the flute. Through a decade of unholy matrimony to a flutist, Roger had many occasions to observe the instrument, to learn of its properties, its qualities, and the techniques associated with its playing.

Some called his ex a *flautist*, but Roger followed her lead in this. "After all," she would say flatly, "I don't play the *flaut*."

Her instrument was something sacred and inviolate to her, the sum of her hopes and fears, her passions and their regulation. Roger acceded to this state of affairs, being an aficionado of music and an amateur guitarist himself. He had decided to marry Bethann after seeing her perform an unaccompanied Bach sonata and knew, without the need of analysis, that Bethann without the flute would not be Bethann.

In reed instruments, it is the thin, vibrating reed that produces sound, amplified by the resonant wood of the instrument's body. In the case of brass, it is the buzzing of the player's tightly pressed lips against the metal mouth-piece. But it is breath itself that accounts for the sound of the flute, a tightly controlled stream of air directed across the mouth-hole of the instrument, bisecting there, some dissipating away, some dancing through the instrument's body, emerging through the keys. Since the mouthpiece offers no resistance to the air stream, a great deal of breath is required to sustain notes. That's why Bethann always forced her beginning students to sit while they played, so they wouldn't fall on the floor when they inevitably grew light-headed. Even for the seasoned professional, breathing presented an ongoing challenge. Bethann's scores were full of markings indicating where it would be possible to take a breath, and Roger was accustomed to hearing her curse composers—normally modernists—whose creations were rife with unbroken passages so lengthy that playing them was practically impossible.

Circular breathing was a technique developed by one of the masters of the previous generation. The concept fascinated Roger, though he had to confess that he couldn't conceive how it could be done; no, he couldn't wrap his mind around it. According to the technique's proponents, it was possible for the flutist to breath in through the nose while continuing to send an outgoing airstream across the flute's mouth-hole. This stratagem would relieve the player of the need to stop playing, however momentarily, in order to draw new breath through the mouth. Bethann referred to the technique from time to time, always clothing her remarks in a healthy skepticism about mastering it—a skepticism which incorporated a mixture of reverence for his abilities, and amusement at his foibles, toward the famous flute virtuoso, one of her mentors, who had pioneered it.

All of these considerations, allusions, inferences and reference points, however, along with the concert schedules, fancy gowns, scores lying about in piles, music stands, publicity brochures, stage fright and ovations, were no longer a part of Roger's world. That all ended the previous autumn, when Bethann waltzed off with a tax attorney she met while playing a concert in Philadelphia. More than a year had passed, though the divorce had yet to be finalized. Roger lived in a one-bedroom apartment near where he and Bethann used to live. After the initial shock wore off, he had managed to put together a new life for himself. It consisted of many things that had made up his life with Bethann, but also much that was different.

A large window occupied the eastern wall of his living room. His desk was in front of it, and when he sat writing in the mornings, he could watch the day dawn over trees that bordered the avenue. Between his building and the avenue was a fire station. On its wide lawn the firemen played noisy games of football in the afternoons. On occasion Roger saw them washing the engines, or running the ladders into the empty sky during drills. A couple of old maples out the window were frequented by chickadees and woodpeckers in the warmer months; all year long crows gathered by threes and fours in the white pines that ringed the firehouse yard, barking noisily for no apparent reason. Tuesday and Friday mornings a truck came and emptied the dumpsters with a great racket. The bells of the Episcopal church across the avenue sounded on the hours. When he lay in bed nights, the swish of cars moving along the avenue reminded him that he wasn't completely alone in the world.

Roger's building was a four-story affair, faced with two different shades of brick. It had been constructed in the sixties, a fact made plain by its interesting shape, marked by bold, irregular angles; by its airy stairwells illuminated by floor-to-ceiling windows; and by geometrically patterned brickwork criss-crossed with veins of concrete. It was an aesthetic (and an era) of happy associations for Roger, and this allowed him to feel that, in some strange way, he had moved up in the world.

His neighbors were a polyglot mix of recent immigrants, old ladies, bachelors, working girls, and welfare mothers whose rent was subsidized by the county. There was a beautiful but troubled Russian who slowly paced the parking lot while she chain smoked, even in the dead of winter. Her downcast eyes seldom met Roger's when they passed in the hallway; a nearly silent hello was the only thing she had ever said to him. Next door was a Filipino taxi driver who once took Roger to the airport. On the way Roger learned that he had two wives, one who lived in the apartment with him and another in the Philippines. He had met number two while working as a guest laborer in Kuwait, and they had come to America together. He happily told Roger about his plans to travel to the Philippines to visit number one and his children. Roger endeavored to share his joy, without revealing the vague apprehension he couldn't help but feel about the entire arrangement.

Upstairs was a young Pakistani couple. The husband, an international economist just starting his career, was taking up a prestigious posting at a global financial institution headquartered in the nearby capital. The wife, with her dark, glancing eyes, was a beauty in her flowing saris, and a pleasant and intelligent conversationalist. Roger would see her around the building during the day, sometimes with her mother-in-law and baby, who completed the economist's household. When she was alone she would stop to chat. "You've got to meet my husband," she would often say. "He doesn't have any friends here."

One evening when Roger encountered her in the hallway she invited him to come right up and meet her mate. She seated Roger on the couch and asked what he would like to drink. After she returned with the drinks, she seated herself across from the men; but her mother-in-law, hovering in the hallway, motioned her out of the room. The husband told Roger about his work and suggested that they go to the movies together sometime. "I really miss going," he lamented. "I used to go all the time, before I got married." It appeared, for reasons Roger could only guess at, that he didn't like to go to the movies with his wife. Perhaps, he surmised, his culture's customs forbade taking her out in public. Unfortunately, Roger wasn't interested in the blockbusters making the rounds of the local theaters, the very movies the husband was keen on seeing. Roger suggested chess, but the husband informed him that he didn't play. Nor was he interested in a hike by the river. After finishing his drink, Roger excused himself.

He continued to see the wife around the building. "You must come to dinner sometime," she would say, though she never specified a date. Roger wondered if he was supposed to simply show up one night. One afternoon, when they were having a friendly chat in the stairwell, the mother-in-law summoned her from the top floor. Roger somehow knew that the mother-in-law didn't really need her for anything. He began to understand that the mother-in-law—the *dueña*—didn't like her son's wife talking with other men. After that he began to avoid her. He didn't want any complications.

No, that was the last thing he wanted.

He amused himself with books and records, staying to himself most of the time. Calls came in from his parents or sister, or from his friend Tom about their mutual business dealings; and from time to time he went into the city to work for their clients. He took walks in the park and occasionally drove over to the river to stroll along its bank. He had a favorite spot there, down through the trees, where the current flooded in among the hummocks and swirled around the submerged boles of maples and oaks. Geese floated out in the channel, and the bank was lined with sweetbrier and morning glory.

He frequented a half-dozen restaurants in the suburban village where he lived on the shores of the city proper. He was on friendly terms with several waiters and even a couple of cooks. On dreary winter mornings he sat in Starbucks with a latte, reading the papers or writing in his notebook. There was a young woman who worked there with aniline hair and delicate hands covered with elaborate silver rings. He liked her innocent, wan way. The manager, Joe, always said hello and asked how "the novel" was going.

On New Year's Eve Roger went to the market for groceries. He was happy to be checked out by a Chinese woman he had known casually—that is, as a simple customer—for several years. He liked that she always smiled and never gave the impression that her work was a drudgery. She greeted all of her customers cheerfully and went about her duties with alacrity. As she handed him his bag full of provisions, they wished one another a happy new year. "Next year," she said, "you have to come back and tell me if it was happy." "I will," he said, "but maybe you won't be working." "No, I'll be here," she said resolutely, cheerful as ever, "I always work holidays." Stepping out into the clear, cold air, Roger felt the year might be worth living. He wondered what it would be like to be married to such a cheerful, Chinese girl.

Not long after New Year's Day Roger filed the divorce papers. The hearing was set for March. Through the heart of that winter he was caught up in an assignment involving long hours, and he barely noticed as the weather raged and then subsided, as the snow piled and then melted. The days were growing longer when the project ended and Roger took stock of his situation. He was aware of an undercurrent of impending change, a sense that his world was making a great revolution—even if it was one that he could only vaguely perceive, much less control. Oddly, he didn't connect this feeling with the upcoming divorce. He felt that he had already been through the worst of it, long months agonizing over how to respond to Bethann's affair. His decisions had been made, and though he didn't doubt that the finality of divorce would bring another—he hoped the last!—adjustment, he had chosen to put it out of his mind. There would be plenty of time later to determine its weight, to assign it some value in his life.

Yet everything around him forced him back upon himself, with a sense of being swept along in an inexorable current toward some precipice beyond which was the unknown. A series of events occurred, trivial in themselves, which taken together focused his attention in a novel way.

He was in the habit of napping at the end of the afternoon. One early evening, after dark had come down like the lid of a big black kettle, he was awakened by a series of unearthly noises coming from the firehouse. He struggled to wakefulness and propped himself on a corduroy bolster, one of two he and Bethann had bought in the early years of their marriage. The noises were overpowering in volume, and impossible to describe without reference to forces of nature or even cosmological events. Though the station's sirens were involved, this wasn't the siren's standard shriek, but rather struck Roger as some stupendous electrical force being allowed, in a controlled fashion, to dissipate in abrupt, wailing chunks—a series of powerful jolts containing their own stunning recoils. As he listened, the phenomenon intensified: now it was the buckling of massive ice floes, or now again the anguished braying of some Paul Bunyanesque water buffalo. Still woozy from sleep, Roger actually said to himself, "But we're not in India!" Finally two tones came into play, one sustaining while the other sounded at close intervals against it. It reminded him of a contemporary piece Bethann once performed, a duet full of quarter tones and impossible rhythms . . .

The slats of the Venetian blinds were cracked, and the headlights of the cars on the avenue cast a constantly shifting pattern against the wall by the bed. Roger watched the horizontal bands of light strobing across one another with a rapidity impossible to follow, blending into infinite shades of gray. He could tell when the light went to red, because the pattern would stabilize momentarily, returning to its ground state. Then, consequent to the revving of the engines, the pattern would begin to oscillate again, a movement both chaotic and mathematically precise. He finally got up from the bed and went to the living room to do some yoga.

The next week he had to drive to the shore to work with a client. When he crossed the Chesapeake Bay the water gleamed like platinum. On the return trip he realized for the first time that the Nanticoke River, which he had crossed many times before, had no real banks. Surrounded by marsh, the watercourse, a flat band lacking either depth or any noticeable movement, spread over the surface of the soaked ground like a spilled liquid. He passed an apple orchard. The crowns of tall, reddish sprouts which topped each tree reached innocently into the sky. A crew of men with ladders and pruning hooks trimmed off the new growth. The clippings lay among the trunks, leaving the ground tinted with apple peel.

The day was ending as he approached Washington. The sun was straight ahead, a huge blazing disk sinking into the city. Its brazen light poured over the highway as motorists sped toward that holocaust, that final disintegration of the day. On the shoulder a man leaned out the window of his car with a camera, recording Armageddon. Roger got on the beltway and headed for home. He passed the hospital where his grandmother had died the previous summer, where the wide pavement rounds a crest before swooping toward the ramp where he would exit. In the deepening dusk, the traffic flooded down the sweeping slope like a river.

With the divorce a week away Roger consulted the *I Ching*. "You cannot avoid the decline that comes AFTER THE END," it said, "yet you can learn to survive such times, and emerge strengthened in spirit and character. Fortify yourself with the knowledge that, with forethought and preparation, even absolute change can be successfully endured." He took a walk down into the park, where it runs along the creek. The shimmering sunlight leapt off the rippled surface of the onmoving watercourse like the life force itself. Later the eastern sky went dark with bands of aquamarine yielding to cerulean; in the west patches of wan light broke through vast, torn rags of gray felt.

When he got out of bed the next morning a yellow quarter moon rose through his window. Everything quavered around him. He went to the living room and sat down to meditate. He had always seen life as a journey toward one thing—the desirable—and away from another—the undesirable; now he realized that he had no choice but to settle into wherever he happened to find himself. He had been accustomed to thinking about life as a struggle against external forces; now he knew that the only important battles would take place within the fortress of his own consciousness. He was newly aware of a strange circularity about things, a perpetual stopping at the same ports, only with the cargo slightly changed each time around. He figured if he could avoid clutching up, if he could keep his mind and senses open and functioning, he could swing it. That's when he started to think about circular breathing: a technique that would allow the wind player—theoretically, at least—to play and breath at the same time. He wasn't sure he thought it possible, but he did like the concept.

The Mask

SOMETIMES HE WONDERED about that painting of Sheri's, the one she tried to give him the day before he left town. But then, so many peculiar things happen in San Cristobal los Angeles, Mexico.

They were in the El Aguacate restaurant, a block over from the Centro on a narrow street not devoid of activity, but quiet enough that Dirk liked to sit at one of the wide, open windows after lunch and watch the afternoon sun spill across the stuccoed walls of the facing buildings, listening to Luis Miguel belt out boleros over the quiet murmurings of whatever scattered guests might still be lingering in the dining room.

On this day, for reasons mysterious to Dirk, the restaurant was still doing an active business, though it was past three o'clock. It could only accommodate a couple dozen people, and Hector was seldom without takers for his *prix fixe* daily special—salad, entrée, coffee and desert, all prepared from the freshest organic ingredients, ingeniously planned, and seasoned in a manner that would not disappoint the most discriminating habitué of the finest eateries of any North American city.

Dirk had arrived later than usual, for this was his last day in San Cristobal; he had spent the morning walking the town's uneven cobblestones to find someone who could safely pack several objets d'art he had acquired during his two-month stay.

He was finishing his desert, and Hector had just come to his table with the cuenta, when Sheri appeared in the doorway. As soon as Dirk saw her there, carrying the large framed canvas in one arm, holding Coco's leash with her spare hand, he knew what she had done. Dirk had met Sheri the year before, in this very spot, when he had made his first trip to San Cristobal los Angeles. He had developed the habit, early in his acquaintance with the town, of frequenting El Aguacate for lunch: for the healthy and ever-changing menu it offered; for its quiet location on the sun-filled, cobbled street; for the nostalgic music that Hector played over his stereo system; but more than anything for the simple, friendly way that Hector and his sister treated their guests. Sheri lunched at the restaurant from time to time, and they met here one day in the simple way North Americans get acquainted in the town, approaching one another with a guileless ease that would be considered a sign of mental instability north of the border. He had learned that she was a widow who had lived in San Cristobal for many years, had two grown daughters in the States and lived not far from the El Aguacate; that though Jewish by birth and sentiment she was involved in a Unitarian church run by some of the local expats, gave English lessons gratis to neighborhood children, and that she painted. She was normally accompanied by her dog Coco, a docile mutt she had rescued from the town's animal shelter.

One day, after they lunched together, she had invited Dirk home to see her paintings. They walked several blocks away from the Centro to a simple townhouse facing the street, painted in one of the earthy shades that predominate in the old colonial town. His visit did not last long; they talked a bit and then she showed him through the tidy little dwelling, every room of which, as well as the hallways, was graced by one or more of her paintings.

One of her efforts in particular affected Dirk, and the two of them stood before it together in a narrow upstairs hallway for some time. Sheri's style of painting was not altogether primitive, though there was about it a directness of both imagery and execution that characterizes art normally given that description. In addition, there was a baldly mystical quality to much of her work (Dirk thought of Redon's *St. George and the Dragon*) which lent it a force which it would not otherwise have achieved.

The painting which arrested their tour through the house depicted a scene from nature; or more properly put, a scene from imagined nature, for Dirk was certain that Sheri had painted the picture from imagination rather than from observation. A solitary deer stood in a meadow bordered by a wood, and a small brook ran through the foreground. Superimposed upon all of this, larger than life and as if floating in the sky, was the face of a young man, his sadly vacant eyes gazing down upon the deer. Dirk was struck by the way Sheri had made the human figure seem to grow out of the landscape, or the landscape out of him, as if the two were lost in a mutual contemplation, one upon which their very existences depended.

They completed their tour of the house and the paintings, and then Sheri offered Dirk a lemonade and told him about her daughters. They came to visit her in San

Cristobal every year or so. One day, she told him, they would inherit her collection of paintings. Each time they visited, she further explained, they took a favorite away with them. Dirk finished his lemonade, thanked her, and went on to his hotel.

Now, when he looked up and saw Sheri coming toward him carrying a large framed painting under one arm, her free hand holding Coco's leash, he knew with certainty that she had brought the painting for him. She had come to the El Aguacate late in the lunchtime hour to find him on his last day in town, aware, as she was, of his habits.

"How very nice of you," he said, after she sat down and told him that she wanted him to have the painting. "But," he continued, "I can't take it. It's too fine. It would probably be worth a good price on the market."

"That doesn't matter to me," she said.

Sheri was well into her eighth decade in Dirk's estimation (though she never made mention of it; nor had she ever spoken or acted in any way that would suggest she thought her age a distinction worth noting). Perhaps her remark was meant to convey, without saying it, that she had come to the realization that all of her possessions, even those most fine, would sooner or later be left behind.

"But it's just too . . . good," Dirk said, at a loss for further words. The fact is, no one had ever made such a gesture to him, and he was dumbfounded. He didn't know Sheri well. They had been friendly in the way two countrymen are friendly when they meet from time to time in a foreign land and share one another's company for lunch. But that was all. How could she offer such a priceless—that's how Dirk saw it, anyway—work of art to a near stranger? And what if, he thought, the painting was a favorite of one of her daughters? What would the daughter say when she next came to town, prepared to claim the piece for her own, and learned that her mother had given it away to someone she hardly knew? She might consider Dirk (he really did think this) some kind of art gold digger, some whippersnapper who had worked his way into her mother's good graces and made off with a family heirloom. He even questioned whether Sheri might not be right in the head, though he possessed not a shred of evidence to suggest that she was anything other than one of the most sane people he had ever met.

At bottom, Dirk didn't have the grace to accept a simple act of unadulterated kindness. Life had not been particularly easy for him, and he didn't trust anything that smelled of an unconditional boon. But he didn't voice as much to Sheri, nor did he let on about any of his other complicated thoughts and emotions.

"Besides," he said to Sheri instead, "I don't see how I could possibly get it back home. I've got to get to the bus depot and the airport with my big suitcase, my frame pack, and five other fragile objects I just had packaged up. The packing stores are all closing now, and I'm afraid that if I were to try to take it as it is I would end up damaging it. Who knows where they would put it on the plane, assuming they would even let me bring in on."

Dirk may as well have been talking to Coco, for Sheri had already adduced that, for whatever reasons, he did not want to take the painting. She did not try to talk him out of his ideas, nor did she suggest any solutions to his supposed difficulties in transporting the piece. Instead she told him in a perfectly neutral voice that she understood and then, after a cordial but brief conversation about other matters, secured the painting again under her arm and she and Coco left for home.

As Dirk sat in the emptying restaurant listening to Luis Miguel clobber an old bolero—*que aunque pase mucho tiempo, nunca olvidaré el momento en que yo te conocí!*[1]—he felt strangely unsettled. He wasn't sure what Sheri thought about his refusal to take her painting; but he didn't think it was altogether good, and he didn't feel that great about it himself. The fact is, he really liked the painting (more than liked it, even; it possessed a sort of totemic power for him) and in many ways he wished that he had accepted it. The face in the painting, that man with the sad eyes, he saw not unhappily as himself. The deer, for reasons having to do with certain esoteric studies he had been involved with, he saw as the more vulnerable recesses of his own heart. The wood, the stream, and the meadow created a benevolent backdrop where these two beings remained eternally locked in mutual contemplation. He pictured how the piece would look on one of the walls of his apartment in Washington, and he reflected that in time he might puzzle out the personal message it so uncannily seemed to bear. But it was now too late. Maybe Sheri would keep the offer open until he could return again to San Cristobal, which he thoroughly intended to do. Perhaps she would even sell him the painting for a not insubstantial sum, if he could get together the funds; that would ease his conscience about relieving her of such a fine piece of work. The whole episode made him feel off kilter, as if life had offered him some grand blessing, but

---

1. "Though much time may pass, I will never forget the moment I met you!"

one which he was too obtuse to profit by.

But as I have written, so many peculiar things happen in San Cristobal los Angeles, that little colonial highlands town, so remarkably preserved, where people still stroll in the jardín in the evenings among the shadows of the ornate cathedral, serenaded by the mariachis' only marginally organized croonings; where Dirk was frequently awakened in the morning by raucous blastings from the marching band at the middle school; where from the terraces of his hostelry he could see, on the ridges to the west of town, the unevenly truncated walls of half-built houses, their owners waiting for funds to complete them; where the townspeople politely greeted one another, and even strangers, when they passed on the narrow sidewalks; where the younger foreigners gathered at La Copa Loca late in the night to flirt and dance to salsa bands; where a little storefront across from Dirk's hotel turned out tortillas by the thousands; and where Americans like himself studied Spanish at the Instituto, painting at the Bellas Artes, and Mexico everywhere.

It was only a couple of weeks earlier that he had gotten involved in the affair of the mask. It started with a chance meeting of the kind he had come to expect when he was in Mexico. He was doing something in his room at the Posada los Angeles when his attention was arrested by the strains of a hauntingly exotic music coming from somewhere without. He left his room and moved along the outdoor promenade that flanked the third-floor guest rooms until he came to one of the wide, flagstone-paved terraces which graced the converted eighteenth-century convent. Seated on one of the wrought iron chairs scattered there, a young man with reddish-blond, short-cropped hair was casually intent upon an instrument that looked like a cross between a lute and a mandolin. Dirk stood aside and listened until the other man looked up and greeted him.

"Very beautiful," Dirk said by way of compliment. "Is that some kind of lute?"

"No," the other said simply, "it's actually a Portuguese guitar." Seeing Dirk's puzzlement, he explained further. "It's been around since the Middle Ages, but today it's chiefly used in fado music."

"Ah," Dirk said. "You play quite well."

The other thanked him for the compliment, Dirk mentioned that he himself played the guitar, and the two talked about music for some time. Dirk learned that the other, whose name was Scott, was a musician by profession, which explained his virtuosity, and that he made his home in California. He was part of an ensemble that composed and played music of a globally eclectic kind, which oddly—Dirk thought, anyway—drew its chief inspiration from the fado tradition of Portugal. Scott's chief partner in this endeavor was a young woman, a singer, who herself had roots on the Iberian Peninsula. Scott explained to Dirk that he and the singer had once been lovers but were now only friends. He told Dirk that they had come to vacation together in Mexico; Dirk was surprised to learn that, in spite of the end of their romance, they shared a room at the Posada.

"Doesn't that cause problems?" Dirk asked.

"Not really," Scott said, eschewing further explanation.

Dirk saw Scott regularly after that, as Scott was in the habit of sitting in the warm altiplano sun to play his intricately woven melodies on the Posada's terraces, many graced with lovely stone fountains. His traveling companion was in the habit of sleeping past noon, Scott told Dirk, so he had much time to kill on his own. Dirk also saw Scott around town, at the jardín or in one of the cafés in the Centro frequented by tourists, and they often stopped to chat. One evening, while sitting under one of the jardín's big laurel trees, Dirk saw Scott approaching with a young woman on his arm. When Scott recognized Dirk he steered his companion toward him and introduced her as Marta, his traveling companion and musical partner.

Dirk had never before seen her. A thin, pale creature with darkly piercing eyes, she clothed herself in a style, with fine layers of garments of different hues and textures, that suggested the same ancient Europe evoked by the music she and Scott performed.

"What are you up to?" Scott asked.

"Just enjoying the evening, watching the ever-changing circus. How about you?"

"We're supposed to meet someone, an artist. I met him the other day at Tio Guapo's. We got to talking, and he invited us to dinner. Hey, why don't you join us?"

"I wouldn't want to horn in," Dirk said. "I mean—"

"Not at all. I'm sure Giacomo would be happy to meet you."

Marta smiled warmly. "Yes," she said, "please come. It will actually make things more comfortable."

Giacomo. Dirk knew who they were referring to. He wasn't acquainted with him personally, but the man's reputation preceded him. As an artist, he was considered a dilettante by the San Cristobal arts community, with several members of which Dirk was acquainted. His lavish lifestyle was thought to be supported by an inherited fortune, and sculpting was how he filled his otherwise idle hours.

Several of Dirk's female acquaintances from the Instituto, having encountered him in the Centro, had found themselves the sudden object of the artist's attentions. He wined and dined a couple of the women in the highest style, and according to their reports owned a large villa among the hillsides to the east of town. Dirk's friend Kathy had returned with him to the place after their only dinner date, but she left when he began to get pushy in what she called a "weird" way. Referring to himself as a "connoisseur of beauty," he had shown her a collection of plaster masks cast from numerous females he had invited to his home over the years, and asked if she might like to take her place among them. Later she pointed him out to Dirk when they sat together in the jardín one day. A strikingly handsome Italian, with stylishly cut graying hair swept back from a high forehead, he cruised slowly around the Centro in a convertible sports car like he owned the world.

Whether out of pure curiosity, because he didn't want to say no to his new friends, or perhaps out of simple loneliness, Dirk consented to join Scott and Marta for their dinner with the man. He got up from his bench and walked with them across the jardín to the nicest restaurant in San Cristobal; situated directly on the town square, its large open windows gave onto a wide veranda. Giacomo was waiting for them at a table just inside one of the windows, and he stood and smiled broadly when he saw them come through the open doors from outside. His smile weakened when he noticed Dirk with them, but he quickly recovered and warmly greeted his two new friends, inquired after

Dirk, and graciously welcomed them all.

Seated at his table was an attractive woman, glamorously dressed in a tight blue dress; the silky blond tresses which spilled over her bare shoulders would have done any shampoo commercial proud. Giacomo introduced her as his assistant, Diane. She stood and greeted the newcomers, and everyone sat down.

"Well," Giacomo started in his buttery Italian accent, "I'm so glad you've come. Now we can just relax and get to know one another."

After they had ordered a round of drinks Giacomo engaged Scott and Marta in a discussion of their music. Scott had given him a copy of their CD.

"I'm so fascinated that you take your inspiration from the Old World," he said. "So many Americans are without any sense of the past. They live such superficial lives. MacDonald's, television." He looked directly at Marta now. "Where you and I come from, there is such a rich culture, passed down over the centuries. Isn't it true?"

Marta smiled noncommittally. Nor did anyone else speak.

"I hope I don't offend anyone," Giacomo said, widening his glance to take in Scott and Dirk. "I exclude present company, naturally."

"Oh no," Scott said politely, while Dirk shrugged off the matter with a gesture of his hand. He was thoroughly acquainted with his own European heritage and believed there was much of it that humanity could have done without: serfdom, the Inquisition, imperialism, fascism . . .

"You're just being honest, Giacomo," Diane said. "The fact is, a lot of we Americans have zip for culture." She sipped long from her cocktail.

"But tell me," Giacomo said to Marta, taking a different tack now, "how does a girl like you find herself following this kind of path—a songstress of ancient melodies, in the land of attention deficit disorder?"

He peered searchingly into her eyes.

"It just comes naturally," Marta said. "Ever since I got into my teens, I found myself drawn to ancient things, old things."

"And how did you get hooked up with this character?" Giacomo asked, taking a jocular tone and gesturing toward Scott.

The conversation went on like this, until Marta turned the discussion to Giacomo's art.

"What about you," she said, "where do you find your inspiration?"

"Such a good question," he replied. Leaning back, he allowed his head to fall over the chair back, taking time to ponder the matter.

"I am always needing to get into the soul of something," he started carefully, when he brought himself forward again, as if still thinking the matter over, "right down to the very heart of it." Here he made an emphatic gesture, pressing the fingers of his hand against the thumb and thrusting it forward. "For there are so many realities possible, are there not?" he went on, as he glanced around the table. "I mean, for each one of us, we can each decide. But I am always wanting to know, deep down within things, if there is not some reality that never changes, something which is the soul of everything."

Dirk heard the mariachis starting up in the jardín.

"The thing is," Giacomo went on, "when I make a sculpture, I have to decide. Because, in the end, the sculpture must end up being one thing. Now I have committed myself. And if I am not careful"—here he looked searchingly at his guests—"I may end up trapped, if you don't mind my using that word, trapped in the sculpture, in a reality that is not real."

Dirk was beginning to feel that he was becoming trapped in a reality that was not real, and he wished that he were strolling in the jardín, listening to the mariachis and watching the passing show of young lovers, kids at the ice cream carts, and old men telling stories. But dinner came and they were soon eating, the food was good, and Dirk had another drink and was glad that he had come. The fact is, he truly liked Scott and enjoyed hearing him now speak of how he came to play the Portuguese guitar, telling also of famous fado players of Portugal and their famous singers; and then Dirk spoke of his fondness for the poetry of Juan Ramón Jiménez, and his mention of Ramón led to a discussion of symbolism and other matters that Dirk enjoyed hearing and speaking about.

When dinner was winding down, with everyone picking at the last remnants of dessert, Giacomo lay down his napkin, fixed his gaze on Marta, and spoke.

"You know," he said, "you have such an interesting face."

She shied away, and Dirk thought he noted a rolling of Scott's eyes.

"Really," Giacomo went on, "a classic face, one that speaks of the ages."

"You're embarrassing me," she said.

"Don't let it bother you," Diane put in. "It's the artist in him. He sees everyone as a potential sculpture."

"Honestly," Giacomo said, "that face should be captured in stone, for others to enjoy." He leaned away from the table, as if gaining ground to take in Marta with greater depth. "It would be quite simple," he said. "All you would need to do is come to my studio one day—tomorrow, for example—and I would make a casting. So you see, you wouldn't need to sit for hours while I sculpt you; no, just long enough to make the cast. Then I would work from there. What do you say? Couldn't I convince you?"

"I'd have to think about it."

"I hope you will say yes."

The waiter came with the cuenta, for Giacomo had arranged for the bill in advance, and after he paid everyone got up and ambled toward the entrance. As they moved onto the veranda, emerging into the festive night of the jardín, Giacomo invited them all to return to his home for drinks and dessert.

Marta and Scott looked at one another and with a shrug of shoulders agreed. Dirk declined, for hearing the mariachis playing, and seeing the big pink cathedral rising up over the square, he was feeling again that he wanted to be away from Giacomo and his affected sophistication, to bask anew in the pure and simple life of this little pueblo that had captured his heart. He parted with the others and went into the jardín, while they walked off toward the side street where Giacomo had parked his Maserati.

The next day, upon returning from the Instituto, Dirk found Scott on one of the Posada's terraces playing his Portuguese guitar. Scott's playing was searingly beautiful, with a deep and deliberate soulfulness; and he was so intent upon it that Dirk stood awestruck before him for some time before Scott noticed him and looked up.

Squinting into the afternoon sun, as if coming out of a dream, he greeted him.

Dirk commented on the mastery of his playing and Scott thanked him.

"How'd it go last night?" Dirk asked.

Scott shook his head slowly. "I don't know," he said, "I just don't know."

"What do you mean?"

"It was . . . weird. Really weird."

"Do you want to talk about it?"

"I'd hate to waste your time."

"I've got nothing to do that can't wait."

"All right. Feel like a drink?"

"Why not?"

The two men went by Scott and Marta's room, where Dirk waited outside while Scott secured his instrument, and then out past the Posada's lobby and onto the street. They walked up Las Aguas to a little café located in a close interior courtyard across from the Bellas Artes. Dirk frequently stopped here for breakfast and had decided it to be one of the most tranquil places on earth. Sun spilled over the stone flagging, and small birds flitted among the bougainvillea that climbed the surrounding walls.

"So, what went down last night?" Dirk asked after the drinks were brought to the table; for Scott sat silently, as if he did not know where to start.

"Well," he eventually began, "we all drove over to Giacomo's place. It's up in those hills that rise to the east of town."

Dirk was aware of the rough location. It was where the wealthiest expats built their palatial homes.

"We hadn't even gotten into the house," Scott went on, "when the first weird thing happened."

"Really?"

"It was getting dusky, and there wasn't much light. The house is big, a two-story contemporary, built into the side of the hill. So as you approach, it sort of looms up before you. And as we drove up, chatting about something or other, a huge cloud of bats came pouring around both sides. They swarmed right over top of the car, and then they disappeared into the night."

"They probably nest in the caves along the hillside."

"That's what Giacomo said. And I'm sure that's true. But it was so gloomy up there, and the house is in such a desolate spot. To tell you the truth, it kind of spooked me. Of course, I was already feeling a little creepy."

"What about?"

"I don't know, maybe about Giacomo in general. There's something about the guy . . ."

"I think I know what you mean. But you went in?"

"Since we'd already driven up there, I didn't feel like we had much choice. I looked over at Marta, and she seemed to take it all in stride. I guess there's no reason I should have expected her to share my paranoia. Besides, she had whispered to me, when we saw Giacomo's Maserati, that we should hit the guy up for some financial backing. Making CDs isn't cheap. He did seem interested in what we've been doing, and he's obviously loaded."

"So how did the evening go?"

"Totally bizarre," Scott said, slowly rocking his head

from side to side.

"Did he show you his mask collection, give you the whole 'connoisseur of beauty' thing?"

"You know about that?"

Dirk told Scout about his friend Kathy's experiences.

"Yeah," Scott said. "He has this room. It's painted all in white, floor to ceiling, like a shrine, and there are nothing but plaster castings of women's faces on the walls. Except in the middle there's a chair, a swivel chair, where he can sit and 'imbibe the beauty,' as he puts it."

"That does sound a little out there."

"I was really creeped out about the whole thing. I told Marta so when we had a moment alone. But she put me off. She always thinks I'm too paranoid, that I worry too much. That's one of the things that didn't work out between us. She's more of a gambler. She tends to take things as they come, without much scrutiny. To be honest, she made me feel like a wimp for being nervous, which really got me down. Screw it, I thought, and I had another glass of wine."

"You were drinking?"

"Oh yes, we were all drinking. First it was wine, then the brandy. Then Giacomo got to asking about our music, and Marta said that she happened to have a rough master of our upcoming CD in her purse. Giacomo asked if he could play it, and she gave me one of her 'see I've got everything under control' looks. We sat listening to our CD for a while, drinking brandy, and it started to feel like everything was going to be all right. Both Giacomo and Diane seemed to enjoy the music. But then Giacomo got back on his thing about Marta's face. He was getting a little drunk now and he wouldn't drop it; the fact is, Marta was getting there, too. Finally she gave me a look like 'what the hell,' and the next I knew we were all going down to his studio together."

"He took the casting?"

"Yes, and that was weird enough. But it got worse."

"How so?"

"After the casting was done, Giacomo looked really pleased with himself; more than pleased, actually. A better word would be *satiated*, as though some deep need had been satisfied. He put the casting on a drying table with a deep sigh. We all went back upstairs then and he started to play up to Marta. He kept going on about her face and how great the sculpture was going to look. We had some other music on now, some rock and roll, and Giacomo practically forced Marta to dance with him. He pulled her off the sofa. Come on everybody, he said, let's party, and he gestured to Diane and me that we should also dance. Marta went along with him, dancing and just sort of fooling around. Maybe she felt attracted to him, or maybe it was just about getting help with the CD. Who knows? For lack of anything better to do, I started to dance with Diane."

"Now you've got a nice little party going on."

"You might say so. But after a couple of songs, Giacomo started to kind of drag Marta toward the hallway, where the bedrooms are located. He was still dancing, but he was pulling her in that direction."

"What was she doing?"

"Whether she was attracted to him or not, I don't think she was ready for that. She looked at me in a beseeching way, trying to resist him, but without being hostile about it. She was trying to coax him back toward the living room. Diane just kept dancing, but her face had taken on an odd expression, like she was purposely zoning out of her environment.

"I was pretty stoned myself, but I had enough presence of mind to know that somebody had to get things under better control. I turned off the music and told Giacomo that I thought he was going too far. 'Too far,' he said, 'how can love be too far?' He took in Diane and me with a broad gesture, and he said that there were plenty of spare rooms in the house, and with a second gesture indicated one of the other hallways. 'So you see,' he said, 'we can all have some fun.' I looked at Marta. She looked scared, but she wasn't saying anything.

"I was jealous, I admit, but more than that I felt like things had gotten out of hand. I told Giacomo that Marta and I had to be going. 'Can't Marta speak for herself?' he said. 'After all, you're not together anymore. You told me so yourself.' I looked at Marta, but she seemed paralyzed. She didn't speak. Maybe it was the brandy, I don't know. I had an urge to take her by the arm and pull her toward the door, but I checked myself. Giacomo was right. We weren't together anymore. Her life was hers, to live as she saw fit.

"What if she was drunk?" Scott went on. "It's not like she was unconscious. I looked her in the eyes and asked if she wanted to leave, but she averted her gaze and wouldn't speak. I stared at her for a long, helpless moment, and then I decided that I couldn't stay in that place any longer. As I headed for the door, Giacomo, from behind my back, offered to call a cab. 'Don't be angry,' he began, but I didn't hear him finish, because I was already out the door. I walked back to the Posada in the dark, following the unpaved roads downward and toward the lights of the town."

"Wow," Dirk said. "Have you seen Marta today?"

"She came in before dawn. She went to the bathroom, and then she crept under the covers of her bed. I didn't let on that I was awake. I didn't want to talk about it. After she drifted off I got dressed, took my guitar and left."

"Will this make things uncomfortable for the two of you?"

"It's not the first lover she's had since we split," he said. "I try to take a Zen approach to these things."

"Expect nothing, seek nothing, cling to nothing . . ." Dirk quoted the great Zen master Dogen.

"Basically."

Dirk told Scott that he had to check into his affairs back in Washington before the day was too advanced, and that he would have to be going. Scott said he wanted to take a walk and the two men parted in front of the Bellas Artes.

"I'll be around if you need me," Dirk said.

Dirk didn't see Scott for several days, until one morning, while he was preparing to leave for his classes at the Instituto, Scott knocked on his door.

"I'm afraid something is wrong," he said.

"What is it?"

"It's Marta."

Dirk invited him in while he finished shaving.

"Marta's never been a morning person," Scott began gravely, "but lately she's begun to stay in bed all day long. When she finally wakes up, she won't talk to me, won't practice. She just sits and stares at the wall. Every now and then she'll start to sing. But it's not our music, or anything I've ever heard. It's nothing but strange, unearthly sounds, and disconnected bits. After I go to bed I hear her go out.

She stays away for hours on end. Usually she doesn't show up again until just before dawn."

"Do you know where she goes?"

"She doesn't say, and I don't want to ask."

"Do you think she's seeing . . ."

"Giacomo?"

"Yeah."

"Hard to say."

"Maybe she's going over to La Copa Loca," Dirk offered.

"I doubt it. Salsa's not her kind of thing."

"Is there anything I can do?"

"I don't know. I'm just worried."

"Do you think she needs a doctor?"

"It doesn't seem to be a medical problem. I believe it's more some kind of psychic imbalance."

"Has she ever had this kind of trouble before?"

"She's always been sensitive, prone to the blues. But the way she's checked out on me, refusing all communication, I've never seen this before."

Dirk had finished his ablutions and had to go. "You'd better keep an eye on her," he said. "Let me know if there's anything I can do."

The next evening Scott intercepted Dirk when he returned to the Posada from dinner. He had been sitting in the lobby waiting for him. They climbed together to the upper terraces of the hotel and sat at one of the ironwork tables. The sun was sinking toward the ridges that flank the town's western edges.

"It's gotten worse," Scott said. "She hardly makes a sound now. And whatever this is, it seems to be taking a toll on her physical health. Her breathing is shallow, as if she's having trouble getting air, and her complexion is deathly pale. When I speak to her, she doesn't appear to even hear what I'm saying."

"It sounds like she may need professional help."

"I wouldn't know who to go to, here in Mexico. Our flight leaves in four days. I'd feel better finding her treatment in the States."

"How will you get her to the airport over in León?"

"I hadn't thought of that. She's so unresponsive."

Dirk had an idea. "Let's talk to Juan Pedro. If we're lucky, we're in time to find him at El Gorrión."

Dirk had met Juan Pedro by happenstance one evening during his first stay in San Cristobal. He was out walking in a section of town away from the Centro, where the streets are dark and deserted in the evenings, when he encountered a blind man frantically, as if he could not get his bearings, tapping his cane along the edge of the curb. The streets and sidewalks are cobbled throughout the town, and the footing is often irregular and treacherous. When Dirk asked the man if he needed assistance, the man replied that he was quite able to manage. But he added that he was on his way to dinner and invited Dirk to join him. Something in his manner told Dirk that he was a man it would be worthwhile to know, and he accepted his invitation.

Over dinner Dirk learned that the man had been born to a peasant family in the nearby countryside; that he had studied at the town's Catholic seminary until his doubts about the entire edifice of Christian belief made it impossible for him to continue in that path; that a tragic love affair resulted in the loss of his eyesight in a manner he chose not to relate; and that he now lived alone, supported by a small stipend from the government. Dirk learned also that Juan Pedro dined every evening at El Gorrión; and due either to his blindness, which made him invisible to those around him, or his stipend, which afforded him the leisure to spend his afternoons sitting in the town square chatting with whomever happened along, there was little that went on in San Cristobal los Angeles that he was not aware of. From that evening on, whenever Dirk needed something, something not otherwise to be found, he looked up Juan Pedro at El Gorrión between the hours of six and eight in the evening.

Dirk and Scott descended through the Posada's overlapping terraces and out onto Las Aguas. They walked up to the Centro and passed through the jardín to the other side of the square. Walking into El Gorrión, they found Juan Pedro eating a plate of spaghetti.

"I see," Juan Pedro said after they had explained the problem. "This could be serious. This man you speak of, Giacomo, I have heard about him. I think he has caused many problems. It is clear from what you have told me that what is ailing your friend is an ailment of the soul. It is as if her world has become twisted, and now something must twist it back into its proper contours. I truly wish none of you had ever gone to that man's house."

Juan Pedro spoke in Spanish; he had to wait while Dirk translated his remarks to Scott.

"That's what I wish," Scott said. "But what can we do now?"

Juan Pedro carefully ingested small, expertly coiled forkfuls of spaghetti while he thought things over. "It is a difficult problem, especially since this man has now captured your friend's image in the mask. If you went to my former masters at the seminary, I imagine they would tell you to pray. You can try that, if you like."

He waited while Dirk translated. "Maybe you should tell him I'm a Buddhist," Scott said, "not a Catholic."

"And the Buddhists," Juan Pedro returned, smiling lightly after Dirk had translated Scott's remark, "I understand that they also pray. Yet I am told that they do not believe in God. I wonder what they pray to. But, to be honest with you, I don't believe that prayer is the answer. In this case, I would recommend something more direct."

"What is that?" Dirk asked.

"There is a lady I know," Juan Pedro began. "She is a curandera. Do you know what that is?"

Dirk, after explaining things to Scott, replied that they both understood that the curanderos were shamans of sorts; that is to say, healers who relied upon traditional methods.

"That is correct," Juan Pedro said. "I cannot of course guarantee that her treatments will be effective, but if I were in your position, I would contact this lady. Her name is Donna María. I can tell you where she lives."

Dirk thanked Juan Pedro and promised to join him for dinner soon. The curandera Donna María lived in the countryside outside of town. Dirk and Scott found a cab and rode out of San Cristobal los Angeles. The cab turned off the blacktop road down one of the dirt lanes along which Dirk was accustomed to watch country people disappear after they disembarked from the regional buses he used when he visited other towns in Guanajuato State. After a mile or so the cabbie pulled up to a dilapidated shack and told the two young Americans that he would wait for them.

The curandera, like Juan Pedro, felt that Marta's condition was a serious matter.

"Her soul is under siege, I tell you," the old woman said emphatically. "The enemy has made an inroad that cannot be taken lightly. If we don't act soon, she may be lost forever." She wanted the young men to bring Marta to her immediately but Dirk explained that, given her listless condition, he wasn't sure how they might coax Marta into the countryside. He asked Donna María if she could come to town with them and see Marta at the Posada.

With a stifled grunt Donna María disappeared into the back of her little home. A few minutes later she reappeared carrying a burlap sack bulging with irregularly shaped objects.

"Lista," she said.

Dirk and Scott were greeted by quizzical looks from the Posada's front desk clerk when they passed the lobby with Donna María. Once in Scott and Marta's room, the curandera looked deeply into Marta's eyes and began to mutter to herself. Extracting a variety of plants out of the burlap sack, and then bundling them with twine, she directed Scot and Dirk to help Marta to her feet and to sustain her there. When Marta was standing Donna María began to voice a plaintive chant. She danced energetically around the patient, stomping her feet and flailing her arms while brushing the bundled plants across Marta's emaciated body—across her back, her front, and down each of her limbs. The old woman lit aromatic herbs and blew the smoke into Marta's face and then had the men lay her on the bed. After probing Marta's belly with her fingertips, Donna María used a hollow tube to blow tobacco smoke onto particular areas; afterward she sucked through the tube, pressing its end against Marta's abdomen. When she had concluded these operations, she turned to Dirk.

"She has been grievously compromised," the old woman said. "That man may say that he is a collector of beauty, but I tell you that he is after bigger game than that! The plants and smoke will help. But as long as that man has the mask, there is only so much that we can do. We will be fighting a losing battle."

That evening Marta came around a little. She responded when Scott spoke to her, and she even sang a few old fado songs with him. But the next day she was once again unresponsive and listless. Her complexion had become deathly pale and her fingernails had turned blue, both signs of dangerously low blood pressure. Scott and Dirk rode out of town to again consult the curandera.

"There is little point in my coming again," Donna María said. "It is like throwing stones at a cloud. In fact, further ministrations from me may weaken her disastrously. It is only the fact that she is resting at the Posada los Angeles, with its holy history, that she has made it this far. There is only one hope for the young woman. You must retrieve that mask! Don't you understand?"

Scott and Dirk rode back to town, and along the way Dirk formulated a plan. He asked the cabbie to take them directly to the house where his friend Kathy rented an apartment. He explained the situation to her.

"It sounds awful," she said. "But I don't know about this curandera business. Your friend's ailment probably needs real medical attention."

"We're just working with the resources at hand," Dirk

said.

"There's got to be a qualified shrink somewhere around here, even if you need to take her over to Querétaro"

"I'm not sure a shrink can help us," Dirk replied. "Juan Pedro thinks it's a problem of the soul."

"Whatever," Kathy said. "I do agree that Giacomo's a jerk."

"Will you help us, then?" Dirk asked.

The plan was simple, Dirk explained. Kathy merely had to visit Giacomo at his studio the following day. She would tell him that she had been overly hasty in refusing his offer to immortalize her features in stone, and that she wanted to talk it over. While she delayed him over a restaurant dinner, Dirk and Scott would have time to break into his house and cop Marta's casting.

All went almost according to plan. The house was easily breached; there were no alarms. But after finding Marta's mask on the wall with the others, something came over Dirk and Scott. They looked at one another and, without speaking, seemed to read one another's thoughts. Circulating about the room, one in one direction, one in the other, they removed each mask from its hook and smashed it unceremoniously under foot. Scott brought the remains of Marta's out with him. He wanted no remnant of her left behind.

They visited the curandera the next day. She was pleased. She performed a small ceremony over the fragments of Marta's casting, using smoke and chants, and then buried the remains in the chaparral behind her shack. Marta's condition began to improve almost immediately; within two days she was coming back to her old self. The

San Cristobal police began an investigation of the break-in at Giacomo's home; but the cogs turn slowly in that colonial town, and before they could get around to interviewing Scott and Marta they had left for the States.

A couple of weeks later Dirk followed them. As he had never been to Giacomo's home, he escaped the suspicions of the local gendarmerie. Giacomo had his doubts about Kathy who, after flirting shamelessly with him over dinner, complained of a headache and walked home by herself, but he could prove nothing.

While riding in the old bus over the dusty roads of Guanajuato State to the airport at León, and throughout his long flight to Washington, Dirk couldn't get Sheri's painting off his mind. Along with all the reasons, practical and emotional, justifiable and spurious, he had adduced for refusing her gracious gesture, he suspected that a good deal of his reluctance to accept the painting had to do with the affair of the mask. He had seen himself in the sad face gazing on the deer at the edge of the wood, as if Sheri had known something vital about him before they had even met; he feared being caught in some magical transaction he was equipped neither to understand nor to guard himself against.

In truth, the painting suggested something that Dirk was not yet prepared to face about himself: like the figure in the canvas, he gazed soulfully upon life, but he had not allowed himself to participate fully in either its struggles or its celebrations. It was the magic of that potential epiphany that both attracted and repelled him in Sheri's masterful work.

It would be several years, however, before Dirk would come to this realization. If from time to time he thought of contacting Sheri to ask her to send the painting, the occasion never seemed right. He was certain that in spite of her air of indifference about the matter he had hurt her feelings in some way, and he did not wish to rub salt into the wound. He could only hope that, should his path ever again lead him to San Cristobal, he would find some way to make it up to her. As of this writing, more than ten years on, he has still not returned to the ancient highland town. But Sheri's painting has worked its magic nonetheless, and Dirk now lives a life more full even than when he wandered the streets of San Cristobal los Angeles like a cloud, watching the mariachis and walking in the jardín, dining with Juan Pedro, and listening to Luis Miguel's boleros as he watched the warm yellow sun of the Mexican altiplano saturate the adobe walls across from the El Aguacate café.

First Governor of Massachusetts

We must delight in each other; make others' conditions our own;
rejoice together, mourn together, labor and suffer together, always
having before our eyes our commission and community in the work,
as members of the same body. So shall we keep the unity of the spirit
in the bond of peace.

John Winthrop, 1630

DOUG WAS A FRIEND of mine. He's gone now. He used to live across the hall in 206.

He was here when I came. I met him in the hallway, outside our heavy, metal doors. Tall and lanky, almost skeletal, with prominent facial bones, he sported big, great ears, and a bushy shock of sandy-colored hair.

"The first governor of Massachusetts Bay," he said with a winning smile, a sort of humble, appreciative pride. He was talking about his ancestors. "My great grandfather was a United States senator, and my great, great . . . great grandfather was the first governor of the Massachusetts Bay Colony."

He batted his eyes in his proud, shy, and winning way.

"I'm real sorry," he said when I told him I was separated from my wife. "I know how it is. My girlfriend left me a year ago. It still hurts." He put a hand over his heart and shifted back and forth, his towering, loose-jointed body rocking like a dead tree in the wind.

"Tell me, Moose," he asked, bending toward me and

taking a confessional tone, "how long were you and your wife together?"

"Nine years."

"That's how long me and Gloria were together!" he exclaimed, taking a surprised step back. "Tell me, Moose," he went on, moving close again, "does it still hurt? I mean, whose idea was it, you know"—I could see he was trying to be delicate—"hers or, you know . . ."

I was caught off guard. His question was pretty personal, considering we had just met. But I let it ride. We had discovered that we were born the same year, and we were both separated from women we had lived with for nine years. Those simple facts created a sort of intimacy between us. Besides, there was something about him that I liked: the boyish manner, the revealing sweetness.

"We were having trouble in our marriage, some of it quite long standing," I said. "We were both frustrated with things." I didn't want to go into any more detail. "But she's the one who broke it off."

"I'm real sorry," he said with a condoling look. "My wife, Gloria—well, she's not my wife, but practically, you know what I mean—she got mixed up with these skinhead motherfuckers. It's her drinking, Moose, that's what did it! Anyway, it's a long story . . ."

"I really miss her," he said after a moment. "Do you miss yours, Moose, your . . . wife?"

Yeah, I did miss her, and I told him so. We were never really right for each other, but she was my friend and now I was lonesome, and clueless about what to do next.

"Well, I'll see you around," he said, chucking his tongue against his teeth and winking a little. He went off down the hallway with his long, loping gait, on his way out of the building. At the stairwell he turned and waved. "Really nice to meet you—Moose," he said with a warm smile, and a manner that would have involved tipping his hat, were he wearing one. He descended the stairs.

I had just moved in. My ex had left a couple of months earlier. I had been living in our old apartment with the remains of our furnishings, a place drenched with sad memories and frustrated desires. The new apartment offered the hope that I might get myself reoriented and put together some kind of better life for myself. The landlady had gone to real pains to make the place presentable. She had the hardwood floors refinished and new Venetian blinds installed. The kitchen floor was replaced with bright new tiles.

Then there was Doug. I considered our meeting a positive omen, given the coincidence of our birth years and our status in regard to women. He seemed a brother, someone inevitable. (In a similar vein, I let myself be encouraged by the name left on my door by the previous tenant—Paz; I kept it there, as some kind of talisman.)

Over the days and weeks that followed I got to know about Doug, about the strange disorder of his life. He said he worked in landscaping, but it seemed he seldom left his apartment. I often heard him over there, across the hall, blasting heavy metal music on the stereo. From time to time the old lady downstairs came up to scream at him through the door. I could hear her smoke-husky voice from my desk. "Turn that goddamn thing down!" she'd rasp out bitterly. Then she would pound on the door, even though she knew he wouldn't answer. "I'm talking to the management," she would roar, "I'll have your ass thrown out of here. Do you hear me? You'd better turn that goddamn thing down!"

The problem with Gloria was that she was an alcoholic. Now she was in prison. "It was that skinhead motherfucker she got mixed up with, Moose, that's what it was. Why couldn't she see it?" He moved closer, taking me into his confidence. "That bastard was nothing but a two-bit pill pusher, but she couldn't see it. He was scum, Moose, scum!"

We were standing in the hallway, where we conducted most of our conversations.

"Nine years, Moose," he said ruefully, "nine years. Tell me, Moose, do you think you'll ever get married again? I mean, I know it's hard to say . . ."

I told him that it was indeed too soon for me to think about making that kind of commitment again. "I know exactly how you feel, Moose," he said. "I feel the same way. I still love her, Moose, that's the thing. I love her—I love her! That's the crazy part, isn't it? Sure there are other girls out there, but I'm not interested. I just want my Gloria back. I'll forgive her everything, if she just comes back to me."

He grew quiet. I said goodbye and began to move away, but he detained me with a gesture of his hand. "Uh, Moose," he said, fumbling with his cig pack, "I've got something to ask you. I hate to do it, but I need sixty bucks—just to get me through the end of the month. Could you, Moose, could you?"

What the heck, I figured. I'd seen plenty of sixty bucks go down the drain.

"You're a pal, Moose, a real pal! As soon as I get my check I'll pay you back. I swear!"

&&&

We're sitting in my apartment. Doug has returned the sixty dollars. I'm in Poang, my favorite Ikea chair. He's in the wicker one, the one that looks British Raj. "Hey Moose, can I talk to you a minute?" he had said in the hallway. "Sure," I told him. "Can we, uh, go inside?" he asked, gesturing towards my place. He leaned toward me. "This place has ears, know what I mean?"

"You see, Moose, all you need to do is write me a check for forty dollars," he told me once we were seated. "Then I turn right around and give you the forty bucks back in cash."

I'm trying to sort it all out, and it doesn't sound good.

"All I need to do is show this guy I'm selling something," he says. "It won't cost you a thing, Moose, you see? You just write a check, then I give you the money back in cash."

He tries to explain it all. "This guy has more money than he knows what to do with, know what I mean? His parents left him a ton, so he bought this Amway franchise." Under his breath he adds, "I think he's gay. I don't think he has any real friends. Of course, I don't know if that has anything to do with it . . ."

He's gesturing with his large, bony hands in front of him, rounded like he's holding a big ball of yarn.

"He gave me a ton of stuff, and I'm supposed to be selling it. By the way, Moose, you don't need any laundry detergent, do you? He's paying me seven hundred dollars every month, as sort of a . . ."

"A draw against commission?"

"Yes, exactly! That's it. Anyway, I'm afraid he's going to

get worried if he doesn't see me selling some of this stuff. Nobody wants it. That's the problem, Moose! Besides, it's expensive. People would rather go to Safeway for their damned laundry detergent!

"All you need to do, Moose, is write a check for forty dollars. Then, here's the other part. I'll give you this guy's number, and you call his machine and leave a message. You say something like, this is so-and-so calling, and I just want to tell you how much I'm enjoying the detergent—or whatever—I bought from Doug. It's real easy, Moose. It's easy. Do you think you could do it? Could you?"

I've already made my decision. I tell him that his scheme sounds like a criminal fraud (I had done a stint in law school) and that I would rather not get involved.

He doesn't press the issue. Nor does he seem particularly crestfallen. "I understand, Moose. I understand. You're a really good guy, Moose. Are you sure you don't need any detergent? Anything? I mean, not to buy it. I've got a whole closet full of the stuff! If you need anything, just let me know. You can have as much as you want—pal!"

&&&

It wasn't long before Doug asked for another loan. We were nearing the end of the month, and once again he sidled up to me in the hallway and asked for sixty dollars. This time he was more loquacious about it, apparently feeling the need to explain himself. He got onto his mother. She lived nearby, in one of the Philadelphia's priciest neighborhoods.

"You see, Moose," he said, talking out the side of his mouth, "normally my mother would help me out a little, but she's strapped too right now. She says she can't do a thing."

"I see."

"Of course, if HENRY needed anything, that would be different."

"Henry?"

"Henry's my brother. Listen to this, Moose, would you listen to this? Henry, my no good brother, lays around the house all day, doesn't do a thing to help, just hangs around the basement playing with his guns. But my mother thinks he's perfect. He's a loser, Moose, that's what he is, a loser! I don't think he's got a single friend. Who is it that worries about my Mom? Who goes over there to help her out, to take out the trash? Me, that's who. But does she see that? No. Listen to this, Moose. Can you believe that a mother would look her own son in the eye and say, I despise you?" Doug's eyes narrowed, as his mother's must have done. "I despise you, I despise you, I despise you! That's what she said, Moose. What kind of mother would say that to her own son? Then she said, I wish you were never born. Can you believe it, Moose? Can you believe it?"

I told him that I indeed found it remarkable.

"She ruined my father, Moose. She threw bleach in his eyes and blinded him. Can you believe that? My father was a lawyer, Moose, a lawyer! He needed his eyes for his work." Doug stood looking at the floor for a moment, slowly hiking his bottom jaw back and forth. "You know, he was quite a guy," he resumed with an air of obvious pride. "He was Bradley's counsel during the Korean War. (Yep, that's my Dad!) Then he was head of the Federal Trade Commission."

Illustrious ancestors . . .

"Is your father still living?"

"No, he died over ten years ago. I really miss him. If he was around now, things would be a lot different, that's for sure."

I was on my way to the gym. I fished sixty bucks out of my billfold and started towards the stairwell.

"Where're you heading, Moose?"

"Over to the Y to work out," I told him.

"Wow, that's great. Hey, how much does it cost there?"

"Forty bucks a month."

"Wow, that's pretty expensive. Hey, Moose, I don't need the gym. Watch, I'll show you something. I get all the work-out I need right here."

He trotted over to the stairway ahead of me. "Watch this," he said. He flipped over like some kind of giant fish, thrust his hands behind him, and caught himself on the third step up. Resting on the heels of his hands, with his knees bent before him, he began to push himself up and down from behind in a sort of inverted push-up.

"This is great for the abs, Moose, great! It's also great for the thighs and calves." He was breathing heavily. His tee shirt had ridden halfway up his midriff, and I could see that the muscles of his almost emaciated abdomen were indeed taut. Then he flipped over again and demonstrated a few normal push-ups.

"Those gyms are a rip-off, Moose. All you need is some steps." He smiled broadly, flushed with the exercise he'd taken.

"Looks like you're in good condition.".

"Yeah, that's from pushing those lawnmowers around. Anyway, I'm not saying you shouldn't go to the gym. You're obviously in pretty good shape yourself. Hey, Moose, thanks for the loan. I'll pay you back the first of the month. You're a real . . . pal—brother!"

&&&

His apartment is an unholy mess. He has invited me in to show me something, or maybe he wants to tell me something. ("Listen, Moose, I'd rather not talk out here in the hallway. Those African bastards down the hall are always poking their noses out the door. They listen to everything!") All is disorder. It's a studio apartment, with an ell to one side; his queen bed is situated there, covered with junk. The living room area contains a hodgepodge of broken down, secondhand furniture. Pride of place is given to the new stereo system I helped him set up after we hauled it from the car a month earlier. It's right in the middle of the floor, like a display model at a store. Peering out from its black lacquered tower, it exudes power: a rock n' roll temple of anarchy; a ziggurat of mindless, heavy metal energy!

Two cats glide across the floor. Sometimes when Doug talks with me from the doorway of his apartment they make a break for the hallway—especially the male, Satchmo. He runs up the hall, flops down, and rubs his back luxuriously against the green carpeting. He allows himself to be captured without a struggle. I rub his belly and bring him back. When Doug is in a bad mood he loses his patience with him. Then I hear him yelling in the hallway. "Godammit Satchmo, you'd better get your ass back in here or . . ."

Is it my imagination, or are the cats now peering up at me with a look that says, "please get us out of here?"

There are plates on the floor with the remnants of old

69

frozen dinners. Aside from the stereo, the most prominent piece in the living room is a big, secondhand stuffed chair. Its green upholstery is faded and frayed. I notice that the wide armrests are covered with small, dark, and shiny craters, cigarette burns in the fabric. It appears that Doug puts out his butts right on the chair. The surrounding carpet is also pocked with burns. There are no drapes on the window, and the blinds hang in disarray. Along one wall is some cheap shelving with a disorderly collection of books and magazines.

&&&

Doug has had an accident. The Mercury is totaled. He's deliberately vague about the circumstances of the crash. His arm is in a sling and there are band-aids on his face, but he doesn't appear to be seriously injured. He needs sixty dollars.

I'm beginning to get the idea about Doug. After the second loan of sixty dollars I had begun to wonder. It was always near the end of the month, and always sixty dollars. The part about the end of the month was understandable. Doug received a disability check the first of every month. It was mailed to his mother. That was the chief source of his income, along with the Amway scam and the occasional lawn mowing job. But why sixty dollars?

It sounded like the right amount for a fix.

I decided to confront him with my suspicions. "Doug," I said, "do you have a drug problem?"

"Yeah, I do." He hung down his head. He couldn't lie to me. He wasn't that kind of guy.

"Do you want to talk about it?"

He told me about the prescription pain killer he used to keep himself feeling good; and then, without instigation on my part, he went through the entire resumé of his psychiatric treatments. His mother had repeatedly had him committed. "She told them I threatened her, Moose, but that was a lie. I'd never threaten my own mother!"

For good or ill, I believed him.

He wasn't interested in any further attention from the medical industry, he told me. They had labeled him manic-depressive and thrown the whole pharmacopoeia at him. But nothing they had to offer gave him the feeling he was looking for, a feeling of simple peace and satisfaction. "With dilaudid, Moose, it's not like I'm drugged. It just makes me feel normal. See, it's not a drug, it's medicine. It's the medicine I need to be normal!"

The problem was, Doug couldn't find a doctor to see things his way and write a prescription for the dilaudid. So he learned to get it on the street. That's how he got mixed up with the pill pusher, the one his Gloria ran off with, eventually landing herself in jail. They would go to an open-air drug market in one of the city's rougher sections, drive up to a guy on the curb who sold the pills for an outrageous price.

I decided to stop lending Doug money. Instead I gave him pep talks. I would allude to his illustrious New England ancestors. I urged him to resume his classes at the community college. I told him that I thought he had smarts, and that I was sure he could do anything he wanted to if he simply got off dope and made an effort. He wanted to get a degree and go to law school like his father had. I let myself believe that, with a little encouragement, he might make a new start.

We talked now and again, or he would knock to get change for the laundry machines, or a few bucks for cigarettes, which I did not begrudge him. Sometimes I would see him out and about, looking sporty in his worn leather bomber jacket. I soon recovered from the illusion that he might stop taking pills on my advice. "Moose, one of these days you'll have to come up to the farm in New York," he would say. "I'll have to make sure HENRY's not using it, of course."

"You're a real pal, Moose, you know that?" he would say. "You're my real brother, not HIM."

He was delighted when he purchased another car at an auction. It was a big Chevy, a cashiered police cruiser. "Isn't it a beauty?" he said, real excited. It was a lush summer evening. The sedan looked sleek and powerful. "Hey, Moose," he said, drawing me aside, "it's got the full police package, know what I mean?"

I did know what he meant, and it made me nervous.

"You want to take a ride? Do you Moose?"

We went flying over far flung suburban roads spread with the cool shadows of a long summer evening. Doug was really living, his hair blowing in the fresh air that streamed through his open window, the stereo cranked with Chicago's first album. From time to time he looked over at me.

"What do you think, Moose? It's great, isn't it!?"

It was good to see him feeling happy.

&&&

When autumn came I left for an extended journey outside the country. I must admit, I didn't think much about

Doug while I was in Portugal, swept up as I was in that ancient country's many wonders. The anniversary of my separation was approaching, and in anticipation of the upcoming divorce hearing, I had taken a month to put the whole sorry business behind me.

A week after my return I still hadn't seen Doug. I was sitting in my chair reading when the knock came at the door. I got up and opened it. There he was in the hallway, bruised and battered. One eye was terribly swollen and contused. He was doubled over with pain, and he held his side at kidney level. He balanced his weight on one leg.

"Doug!" I asked, "what happened?"

"I . . . had an accident," he sputtered, completely bedraggled.

"Where . . . when?"

"Oh, I don't know . . ." He winced with pain and gripped his side more tightly.

"Have you seen a doctor?"

"Yeah, they took me to the hospital."

"What did they say?"

"They, uh, took some x-rays. Nothing was broken. But the steering wheel rammed my stomach and bruised my kidney."

"What's wrong with your foot?"

"Ouch!" he said and grimaced fiercely. He bent over further. "I don't know? It's sprained or something."

He wasn't wearing shoes or socks. The foot was purplish red and swollen. It looked like a big eggplant stuck on the end of his leg.

"You'd better keep an eye on that. Do you need anything? Is there anything I can do?"

"Look, Moose," he said, "I hate to ask, but could you lend me a hundred dollars?"

I hesitated.

"The pain is killing me, Moose. Ouch! That damned Tylenol's not doing a thing!" He looked like he was about to faint. I went into my apartment for the money.

Over the next several days I periodically knocked on Doug's door. He would not answer, though I knew he was in there. Often the stereo would be playing loudly. I pictured him sitting in the tattered easy chair, floating in a narcotic haze, cig butts searing into the upholstery or the carpet, threatening to burn the building down.

One day he knocked at my door. When I opened he was standing in the hallway in his tightie-whities with an obscene-looking rubber tourniquet tied tightly around his arm at the elbow. He was even skinnier than usual, really wasting away. His swollen foot was growing larger.

He wanted me to pick him up some cigs.

"You need to see a doctor about that foot."

"Yeah, I know," he said hazily. He was very stoned.

"You need to do it soon—like now. I'll take you tomorrow morning, first thing. Is that all right?"

"All right, pal," he got out. "You're the best, Moose. You're the best friend a guy ever had."

The next morning I knocked on his door for five minutes: no answer. I made several more attempts in the afternoon, but there was still no response, though the stereo boomed on with its relentless, crazed surging. Each time I knocked the cats put their noses to the crack at the bottom of the door. I figured they hadn't been fed for days. I was agitated. Should I call for an emergency squad?

But if I did, wouldn't they find the contraband dope?

Later that evening he finally came to his door. I told him that we were going to the hospital the next morning, period. I could drop him off on my way to work. He had to cut the bullshit, I told him, or he was going to end up without a foot, maybe without a leg.

He weakly agreed.

When I came to collect him in the morning he tried to put me off. I went into his apartment and assured him that I wasn't going to leave without him. I made him put on his clothes and spoke to him like a child. "Okay, where's your shirt? Do you have a clean shirt?" He hobbled around, wincing and moaning, trying to pack things into a ragged gym bag. I did good-cop, bad-cop, but I had to play both parts. "Look, no more crap, Doug. This is serious. Get your stuff and quit stalling." Then, in a conciliatory tone, "Don't worry, everything's going to be okay."

"I'm coming," he kept saying, "I'm coming!"

Finally I took him by the arm and led him to the parking lot, got him into the car, and maneuvered out onto the avenue. Before we had traveled two blocks he got cold feet.

"Look, Moose, I don't think this is such a good idea."

I knew what the problem was. He was afraid the hospital would refer him to the authorities for placement in detox. He had been there before. We were at a red light not far from the fire station. He started to fumble with the door latch—as if he were capable of walking away on his own. I didn't have time to fool around. The television crew I worked with in those days was waiting for me downtown. Fortunately, the light turned green. I stepped on it before Doug could get the door open and whipped into the station's drive. I went into the office and addressed myself to the captain.

"I've got a friend in the car there," I said. "He had an accident the other day and his foot is very swollen. He needs medical attention. He's got an intravenous drug habit, and he doesn't want to go to the hospital."

"Okay," the captain said, "we'll take care of him."

I stood by while the paramedics brought up the wheelchair. Doug did not resist. He respected firemen too much for that. I handed off his gym bag and headed for work.

I didn't hear from him for a couple of days, until he called from the hospital. They had taken care of the foot, but the situation with the kidney had deteriorated. They were going to have to remove it. He asked me to look after the cats. He was anxious about the operation.

"Don't worry," I told him, "you can live perfectly well with one kidney. Lots of people do. Everything's going to be all right."

After the operation he went to his mother's house to convalesce, but he continued to stay there long beyond the time needed for recuperation. From what I gathered from his phone calls ("Hey Moose, can you bring me some cigarettes?") and my occasional visit, he had become deeply enmeshed in a byzantine struggle with his brother over his mother's favor. Chiefly, he was afraid that Henry would angle him out of his inheritance.

"Can you believe it, Moose? He already acts like the farm belongs to him!"

I tried to convince Doug to forget about his mother and his brother and to make a life for himself, but he wasn't buying it. I came to understand that his master life plan called for waiting out the death of his mother, so that he could coast through the remainder of his existence on the legacy that his New England ancestors had built.

I began to do some looking into the early history of Massachusetts. I wanted to know if Doug's assertions about his ancestry were true and, if so, what sorts of deeds his heroic forefathers had accomplished.

I consulted several sources. It was easy to determine that the first governor of Massachusetts Bay Colony did not share Doug's patronymic (Parker); for that would have been John Winthrop, who famously led the first colonists to the Bay Colony with admonitions to build a City on a Hill. The welter of possible connections through maternal lines of descent, however, defeated my efforts to bring the question to some definitive resolution. I was able to determine that a man bearing Doug's surname was involved in King Philip's War, and that another served in the United States Congress shortly after the Revolution. Who knows, perhaps one of his ancestors was the first *something* of Massachusetts, and through those circuitous maternal lines, maybe even governor. His mother's maiden name is represented among the "old two hundred," those earliest Puritan settlers who considered themselves the bedrock of New England history. Admission to the society required written testimony that the applicant's character was "perfectly unvarnished, that he be a moral and industrious man, and absolutely free of the vice of intoxication!"

I've lost track of Doug. He had to give up the apartment, and as he recovered from his operation he had less occasion to call ("Hey Moose, can you bring me some cigarettes?"). For my part, I thinned out my visits, repulsed as

I was by the atmosphere of toxic intrigue that permeated the mother's household—the household of a modern day Clytemnestra, presiding over the fall of a once great line. I did learn that Gloria, upon her release from prison, returned to my friend. She moved into the mother's house, where she fortified Doug in his internecine struggles with Henry. When I ran into them at the Safeway one day Doug seemed happy and carefree, a sign that he was getting his "prescription" filled. Gloria talked about finding an apartment of their own.

I'm hoping for the best.

To the Ends of Space

SHE LAY AWAKE nights. It really wasn't so bad; it had been years since she'd slept much. She used to go into the office before dawn, when she was still working, so she could get some things done before the Judge came in with his grouchy moods and helpless entreaties. Now that she was retired there was hardly any reason to turn in at all, though of course a body needed some shut-eye to "keep the machine running." There were so many things to think about, what with Social Security in trouble and war and the dumming down of America, besides things that would pop into her mind at random, like the awful divorce—or even worse catastrophes, from still longer ago. Then it was a good thing for the radio. It not only kept her company, as she lay without a shred of drowsiness (half-curled against three pillows, her satiny covers pulled up to her chin), she could also keep abreast of the nation's ills thanks to the wonders of talk radio. Sometimes, though, all that opinion-ated jabbering made her feel even less like sleeping. Then she would zero in past all the static and weird frequency sounds until she heard the sonorous voice of Jack Kestle broadcasting, as he said in his introduction, "TO THE ENDS OF SPACE . . ."

Along the hallway that leads from her front door to the

living room are mounted two large bulletin boards. They're freighted with photographs that cover every square centimeter of cork—family on one, friends on the other. When her second son Dexter came by with his friend Dilip one day she stood in the hallway and conducted a tour through this labyrinth of relationships. "That's my brother Ralph,' she said to Dilip, pointing at a photograph on the family bulletin board. "He died from a brain aneurysm last year. Nobody knew there was anything wrong with him. Got up one morning to go to the bathroom and just collapsed." She shrugged, shuffled sideways a little and pointed again. "This here is my mother,' she said, "she died a few years back."

"I'm sorry," Dilip said.

Peg stepped away, as though she will still registering the news of her mother's demise, and then she again perused the board with her eyes. "Oh, there's Dexter with Robert's oldest," she said, more lively now. "They've always been close." She approached the board and scanned her hand across its surface until lighting on another photograph. "This is my son in Florida with his little one, cute little thing. And here's my daughter and her little sweeties." Her face lit up. "You should see when they come to visit, they're all over the place—in the bathroom, my bedroom, climbing over everything. You've got to keep them entertained, I'll tell you that!"

"Who is this?" Dilip asked. He pointed to an ancient black and white image with scalloped borders. Two young women in calf-length, belted dresses stared out at him, one with a toothy smile, the other with dark hair and flashing eyes. Their arms are around one another's waists. Behind them sits a little white bungalow.

"That's me and my sister," Peg said flatly. "She died when we were young."

There was an awkward silence, but Peg was already padding over to the "friends" bulletin board to resume her narrative. "That's my friends Don and Carla," she announced, bracing her broad teeth into a tender smile as she pointed out an older couple in fancy dress. "He's got Alzheimer's, poor thing. They had to quit coming to the dances."

"That's too bad," Dilip said. Peg shuffled over a little.

"This is Betty," she went on. "She roomed with me on the cruise last year. She's got diabetes real bad."

"Oh."

"There's Dick and Sally," Peg said, pointing again. "He's gone now. These two are gone." She tapped a cruelly bent arthritic finger to one photo after another, all over the friends bulletin board. "She's gone. They're gone. He's gone. It's like I told Dexter, if there's anything you want to do, you had better do it now!"

A week before Peg had gotten a letter from her ex-husband, the father of her children. It seemed odd after all these years. It happened so long ago; and now, with both of them well into their seventies, couldn't he just forget it? "Dear Peggy," it said, "Since I retired I've had a lot of time to think about things. Overall I'm pretty content with my life, except for that one big mistake I made. I won't rehash the gory details. That would be too painful for both of us. You were the best thing that ever happened to me. I hope you know that. I'll never forgive myself for what I did. I don't deserve it. Having said that, it may seem odd that I'm writing to ask *you* to forgive me. We're older now, and I feel it would be helpful, maybe for both of us. I'm certain I could rest easier if I knew you understood how profoundly sorry I am for the pain that I put you, and the rest of our family, through. I hate to say it, but we may not be here much longer. I've done my best since our break-up to be the kind of man you helped to make me. Please forgive me, and let me face what's coming all too soon with a lighter heart. Yours, Richard."

She couldn't help notice that his hand, like hers, had grown shaky over the years. She wanted to cry but confined herself to a few filmy tears, a mere wetness over the eyes. "Oh Richard," she said to herself, and she pictured him sitting in his Florida golf home with nothing better to do than write letters about thirty years ago. She set the letter on the bureau and decided not to give it much thought. Of course she had forgiven him, hadn't she? There was never any unpleasantness at family gatherings, and she never talked him down to the kids. "These parents that put the kids in the middle," she would say to Dexter, "I think that's horrible. That's why I never did that with you all and your father." She didn't begrudge him his own happiness.

She had moved on.

There were so many things to do. It wasn't like she had hours to sit around and ruminate about the past. That mess on the enclosed porch, for example: all those boxes of old photos and things, including the load she had brought out from her mother's place after she died. That's not to mention the endless administrative work for the dance club, or the small library of papers about the condo, and insurance, and Medicare, and on and on and on. At least she had her secretarial skills to fall back on. That was one good thing.

As soon as she got some time she meant to make each of her children a special album, using the photos from the porch boxes along with other memorabilia she had held on to for years. It felt like some kind of sacred responsibility, something she should take care of before she went the way of so many friends on the bulletin boards in the hallway . . .

She lay awake nights. Things would float into her mind at random. Then, just as randomly, they would float out. At times like that it was a good thing for the radio. That Jack Kestle was quite something, always smooth and polite, and so curious about everything. All the way from the high sierra, imagine! And the things he delved into—no wonder her dance club friend Charley Haddock had recommended it. She had overheard him talking about the famous seer Edgar Cayce at one of their dances.

"I used to like to read about that kind of thing," she chimed in, "and Bridey Murphy, reincarnation, all that. Of course, that was back of a day." (*Back of a day* before she married, when she could save and scrimp and ride a train with her girlfriend Annie Rooney all the way to Miami Beach. Weren't they something!) "You've got to listen to this guy, Peg," Charley Haddock had said. "He's got the real stuff." So she figured she ought to try it. And that very night she turned against her propped up pillows and switched the radio to the a.m. part, slowly homed in past all the weird static and funny radio sounds and there, suddenly, clear as a bell, was Jack Kestle interviewing an alien abductee . . .

"Now you know," Kestle was saying, "just to be honest here, and I'm sure you've heard all this before, but the average person might think you weren't quite right upstairs. No offense—you know how open-minded I am about this kind of stuff—but do you often get that kind of thing?"

"Of course, Jack, all the time. You know how it is." The abductee was a woman named Joan. She claimed to have been transported (several times) from her bedroom in a shaft of brilliant light to another realm where she enjoyed ecstatic sexual experiences with a reptilian inter-dimensional being.

"If you don't mind my asking," Jack said, "and I realize this is pretty personal stuff, but what was it like? I mean, how did it feel? Are you okay with this?"

"First of all, Jack, I'm okay. I mean, if we were sitting here talking about some guy I met at a bar last week, this would just be some kind of kinky voyeurism. But what we're talking about has implications for all of us as we move into the next millennial cycle. I feel my task here is to share this knowledge as widely as possible, so that we can start to prepare ourselves."

"I see," Jack Kestle replied in professorial tones. Then he continued more eagerly. "But let's get back to basics. What was it like?"

"It was simply like nothing I've ever experienced before," Joan said. "There was total love and connection, without words or even the need for them. I felt engulfed in the presence of some . . . thing, one, who understood my every need."

"That's pretty extraordinary, especially in this day and age," Kestle remarked. "But give us more details. I mean, what did your lover—can we call him that?—look like? What did he *feel* like?"

"As I've said, he was definitely one of the reptilians. Rather tall. His scales were soft to the touch, but he was firm and muscular, quite strong."

"Scales?! Wait, you said strong. Did he overpower you?"

"I don't know," Joan said coquettishly, "I can be pretty assertive myself in some areas. . . ."

"Hmm, I think we had better let that one lie. But what about the overall structure? Was he humanoid? I mean, two arms, two legs, all that?"

"Yes, two arms and legs."

"And the face? Human?"

"More or less. He has these beautiful green eyes, very searching. There are no ears, and the nose is flattened. The tail's about four feet . . ."

"Hold the phone! This thing had a tail?"

"Of course," Joan said.

"You know, Joan, a lot of people might say, 'You got into bed with that?'"

"Jack, I think a lot of men would say that. But I can't tell you how many women have told me that they would love to have the experiences I've had. Women aren't so visual. For us, the emotional content is much more important."

"Okay, I know this is sensitive. You're a lady and all that. But could you compare it to doing the do with an earthling guy?"

"Well—"

Joan hesitated, and Peg knew that she was smiling. She could hear it in her voice.

"Go ahead," Jack said, "you're not going to wound anybody's feelings."

"I'll just say what I've said before. It was like nothing I've ever known. There was a level of trust I have always sought with my own kind, but never found."

"It was better," Jack said.

"I didn't say that."

"But it was," he persisted. "I can tell."

"Okay, then," Joan conceded, "it was."

"Goodness!" Peg thought, and she pulled up the covers more tightly.

Joan let out a little laugh.

"Was it a matter of technique?" Jack Kestle asked.

"You're such a typical earth male."

"What do you mean by that?"

"Technique's important, sure. And this guy was no slouch in that regard, let me tell you. But we women are more into intimacy, a sense of connectedness. And you've got to realize, there was something else . . ."

"Something else?!"

"Yes. You see, I was made aware that this being and I have been together in other incarnations."

"That's fascinating, and I want to pick up on that. But wait a minute. You keep saying 'this being.' Frankly, that seems awfully cold, after where the two of you have been together. Doesn't this thing have a name?"

"Jack, in this realm, names aren't necessary. Beings recognize one another through pure feeling, a sort of soul memory."

"Soul memory? Okay, so this 'being'—are you sure we can't call him something? How about 'Lizzy,' or 'Slithy?' Maybe Mr. Komodo?"

Joan laughed again. Peg smiled broadly; she thought it was funny, too.

"All right," Jack resumed in his reporter's voice, "you were 'made aware' that you knew this reptilian being in other incarnations."

"That's right."

"And how were you 'made aware' of this? Did Lizzy speak to you?"

"Language isn't used in this realm, because it isn't needed. I would call it telepathy, but it's more direct than that. It's like knowing one another's thoughts as they occur."

"I see. So he telepathically, or whatever you want to call it, imparted this information to you—this information about your former lifetimes together?"

"Actually, it was more impressive than that. In the middle of, you know, I experienced an overwhelming vision of a time and place when I was with this being. We were on the crest of a hill, surrounded by others of our own kind, and all of us were peering into the infinity of space. We were bathed in a shaft of pure, white light."

"Do you know when this incarnation occurred?"

"It was many cycles ago, hundreds of thousands of years in our time reckoning."

"I see. But why would Lizzy contact you now?"

"That's the very heart of what this is all about. You see, in our former incarnation, the two of us were leaders. At that time the planet was reaching the apex of a spiritual cycle, a time when all beings become aware of their basic unity. It was a time of oneness and peace for all, and we two had been instrumental in gathering others into that awareness. It's my belief, based on scads of teachings, that humanity is approaching that kind of cycle again. And I believe that I've been contacted by my former soul mate to be reminded of inner strengths that I have forgotten, potentials that I will need in order to help my fellow beings transition into this new era."

"Joan, I've got to ask, are you dating anyone, and what does he think about all of this?"

They carried on their conversation, touching on Joan's many abductions by the grays, her experiences with astral travel, and her harassment by the men in black, until Peg grew woozy and fell into a deep slumber. She awoke in the morning feeling lighter than usual, and she went about her normal business of sifting through things on the porch and papers on her dining table. Although she didn't give much thought to the previous night's radio show, now and then, as she made her way through the rooms of her condo, a strange vision filled her mind: a vision of radiant light, a hilltop and vague figures straining toward the sky . . .

That's how she got hooked on Jack Kestle's radio show.

Her gentleman friend Bud called to pick her up. They were going to a dinner dance together. They stood in the hallway by the photographs on the bulletin boards. Bud was helping her on with her coat. He was courteous like that.

"Did you ever listen to Starlight Radio?" she asked.

"That weird stuff Charley Haddock's into? Lord, no."

"Oh," she said.

"Why do you ask?" he inquired after a pause, aware that his response had put a damper on their conversation.

"Oh, nothing."

She was getting bottled up in herself, and it made him nervous.

"Isn't it about UFOs and reincarnation, and stuff like that?" he asked as respectfully as he could, trying to get some kind of flow going.

"I don't know much about it," she replied curtly. "I've only listened once or twice, out of curiosity."

"I didn't mean to say there was anything wrong with it ..."

"I know," she said.

But that was the last time she would bring up Starlight Radio with Bud. She had calculated, in the years after her divorce, that if there had been anything positive about the whole scenario, it was that she no longer had to put up with the peculiarly condescending quality of the male ego. Bud was a nice man and a gentle one, cut from a different cloth than her macho ex, and she knew that he was sorry he had sounded dismissive. But she couldn't risk it. She changed the subject as they walked to the car, friendly gossip and dance club business, and the ingenious projects in which Bud's son was forever involving himself. This was how she preferred to keep things with Bud, as she had with all the men she had dated since her divorce—"polite and light." There was to be no more *sturm und drang* for her; she had had enough of that with her children's father, and in struggles with other men before their lengthy marriage. Now more than ever, as she saw the end of her life drawing near, she wanted only to enjoy herself and to live in peace.

One night she lay awake. Jack Kestle was interviewing someone who called himself a shamanic astrologer. The astrologer, who's name was Ben Eagle Soaring, said that we were approaching the end of a cycle, just like that woman Joan had said. This only happens once every twenty-six thousand years, according to Ben Eagle Soaring.

"One thing I think many of us are aware of during this period of transition," he went on, "is a sense of accelerated time, and a compression of events. This is a time when psychic evolution can take place at an amazing velocity. Look at divorce, for example, and all the relationships people are having today. Unlike many, I don't see this as some kind of social breakdown. Rather, it's just that people are completing the work they need to do in these intimate partnerings far more quickly, and moving on to other relationships where they can continue to grow. It's like living many lifetimes in one life span."

"Hmph," Peg grunted softly, adjusting her slight weight on the propped up pillows, turning down the radio. She looked toward the bureau, where the letter from Richard still sat. "Dang silly fool," she said to herself. What was the point of rehashing? The main thing was to keep moving. Life's for the living, isn't it?

She slept funny that night.

Her days were filled with sorting and sifting. Now she was neglecting the papers about the condo and insurance, and more and more spending time putting together the memento albums for her children. She vaguely recognized that a turning of some kind had been reached, merely by the fact that she could handle photos of the happy years of her marriage—her and Richard with the kids, at the beach or the mountains—without any sense of self-betrayal or even loss. How simple they were, with such hopes and ambitions! This she now observed with quiet wonder, even a sense of gratitude at having once been so innocent. Now she understood what it comes to in the end: the relentlessness of aging and, if you're lucky, good friends and some memories you can live with.

What was more difficult were the photos she had brought from her mother's place, black-and-white images that went back to her Depression-era childhood. There she saw her in so many guises (the two of them playing together as children, or showing off in new outfits, looking glamorous in that swing era way) and one of those griefs she had never subdued struggled to break from its cage and cleave through its dark sky toward a place where such things can live in peace and freedom. She was caught with the sudden sensation that she was behindtimes with regard to Mary's death; she had never really dealt with it, she realized, and how much time remained?

But how could you deal with such a thing; what can you say, think, or feel when your only sister blows her brains out with a sawed-off shotgun, leaving all her loved ones, including an infant child, behind? It was her emotional nature, Peg's brother Rodney had said, an unpredictability that always delighted Peg with whimsical high spirits, but also terrorized her with black moods and silent spells. Inwardly Peg had blamed herself. When Mary became depressed after the birth of her baby, Peg had meant to stop in on her more often. But with so much to do to keep her own brood going, it seemed there was never any time. After the initial trauma, she had just numbed it away. She had to keep stepping for the sake of her family. She remembered, and was wordlessly thankful for, Richard's pig-headed strength, without which she might not have made it through.

She was on the enclosed porch, sorting the photographs in the boxes; outside the glass doors, a sun-washed wintry day seemed to stop time. She began to feel lightheaded and feared she had let her blood sugar run down. She struggled toward the sofa in the living room, clutching a handful of photographs. She lay back and pulled a pillow behind her head. "Oh mama," she said, allowing the photos to drop to the floor as she drifted into a dream. She was with her mother at the nursing home before she died. Her mother knew that she didn't have long to go. "It's awful nice here," her mother said, "but this is no way to live. I never know where I am half the time. I can't even recognize my own grandkids! It's embarrassing." Peg lightly patted her hand. "I'm going home soon," her mother said, "home to Daddy and Mary." Peg strained to speak, but she couldn't make the words come out. Where was her mother going? she wanted to know. Where was she now? And where were Daddy and Mary, and her brother Ralph? She awoke with a jolt. At first she didn't recognize where she was. Then she saw the sun beyond the enclosed porch, the trail of photographs leading to the sofa. She pulled herself up with a groan and let herself weep awhile.

She had to help organize the St. Paddy's dance, and then her eldest Robert and his wife Doris came by one evening and they went to dinner to celebrate his birthday. Her daughter brought the little ones over and she tried to find things to entertain them the way her own mother used to do with her kids. In between things like this she sorted and sifted, checked in with friends on the phone, went out with Bud, and sorted and sifted some more.

But in the midst of all of this she could not stop thinking about her sister, Mary. Something had gotten set off inside, and it just kept growing like a weed you can't kill if you try. She pictured the little room they shared as girls in the front corner of the old bungalow, and how they would greet one another every morning with the phrase, "What's shakin', bright eyes?" She remembered how they became fascinated with Bridey Murphy, and how they entertained themselves making up stories about their own past lives as Cleopatra, pioneer women, or World War One flying aces. She also remembered double-dating with Richard and Joe, the father of Mary's baby, and that made her think about her nephew and reminded her that she ought to check on him.

One night Jack Kestle was interviewing a psychic named Thomas Van Dorn. Thomas Van Dorn said there were a lot of things we don't understand about the way life is set up. He said there are other dimensions of reality, just like that alien abductee Joan had said. He also said that time isn't a straight line, like we think, but is happening all at once. "Hmph," Peg thought. Thomas Van Dorn further claimed that people are forever popping back and forth from one plane of reality to another.

"You see," he said, "we have work to do on this side, and we have work to do on the other side. We just keep evolving, on whichever plane is best suited to our circumstances."

"I can understand that," Jack said. "But what about the ones who should be on the other side, but they stick around here and don't want to leave? You know, like ghosts?"

"Yes," Thomas Van Dorn agreed, in his gentle manner, "sometimes they do stick around, especially if they have to leave unexpectedly. Let's say they were murdered or something; or an accident, perhaps. Sometimes it's just a part of them that stays around."

"Wait," Jack interrupted, "a part of them?"

"Yes," Thomas Van Dorn replied, chuckling lightly at Kestle's surprise. "You see, we can exist on multiple planes of reality at the same time, through the manifestation of different facets of ourselves, so to speak."

"Okay, fine. But what I want to know is, what should we say to one of these facets, if that's what we're going to call them, who doesn't want to leave?"

"You should just tell them that they would be much better off on the other side. That's where their work is, after all, not here."

"That sounds reasonable enough," Jack said after a thoughtful pause. "Let's just hope they listen." He laughed awkwardly before going on. "So, getting back to basics, if I understand correctly, we're constantly evolving, moving from this side to the other. But how does a soul know when it's time to come back to life in this world?"

"They probably use their intuition, much the same way we make decisions here on earth. And believe me, they make mistakes. Take suicides, for example. I believe that these are people who have come back too soon, before they're ready. They haven't yet finished the work they had to do on the other side, and when they get here, it's too much for them. So, they bail out. This would especially be true of a person who tended to have an impulsive nature."

"Mary!" Peg thought.

"Okay," Jack said to Thomas Van Dorn, "change of topic. Let's talk about the work you've been doing with electronic voice phenomena . . ."

"Ah, yes," Van Dorn purred, "a fascinating area, and one that's getting more and more attention lately."

"Tell us about it."

"It started, with me, in a simple way," Van Dorn said. "It was while I was listening to a cassette tape. Remember those? Anyway, I was driving along the Santa Monica freeway—I remember it like it was yesterday—when something went haywire with the car's stereo system. I couldn't tell you what it was; I'm not the least bit technical. But it was very late at night, the highway completely deserted, when the tape started to make these . . . I'd call them . . . gurgling sounds. I was about to shut the thing off, but there was something about those sounds that was strangely intriguing. And then, after a minute, little phrases started to pop out here and there."

"As if something were communicating with you!"

"It was just a word or two, here and there. But it was very clear, very unmistakable. 'Hello there.' 'How's tricks?' That sort of thing . . ."

"Did you have any idea who—or what—this was?"

"At the time, no. But these experiences began to repeat themselves; and over time, I became convinced that these were voices from the other side."

"Did you know these people?"

"Not always. In the case of the first one, I'm convinced that it was my mother. She had died a couple of years before."

"Mmm, and have you continued to use that same cassette player?"

"Yes, and the malfunction never repeated itself. Odd, isn't it? But after that episode, I became attuned to these transmissions in all kinds of things we normally dismiss as random noise. You know, static on the television, the refrigerator humming. Nowadays more and more people are having these experiences with computers. One that I especially like is that sound the modem makes when it's trying to connect you online."

"You say more and more people are having these

experiences. But can just anyone hear these things, or do you need to have psychic abilities?"

"It's really just a matter of openness and sensitivity. I believe we're all born with psychic talent. Some of us may have more capacity, just as with playing the violin or doing algebra; and some may develop their capacities more; but everyone is born with at least some potential in the psychic realm. Most of us simply never allow these skills to develop because of our restrictive worldviews. After all, you're not going to see or hear something, if you don't believe that it can even exist . . ."

Peg turned off the radio and lay perfectly still. She felt funny, like she wasn't alone. She got up and turned on the bathroom light; and then she cracked the door, so that her room wouldn't be completely dark. Though she pulled up the covers tightly around her chin, she wasn't able to fall asleep for some time, not until she fixed her mind on a field of stars in a dark and endless sky . . .

She was reluctant to listen to Jack Kestle's show the following night, but something pulled her to the radio in spite of herself. And then, while tuning in the station, homing through the funny radio noise toward Starlight's frequency, something so startling happened that she nearly jumped off the bed. She heard a voice, very distinctly, break through the chaos of the radio interference. "What's shakin', bright eyes?" it said. She turned on the light and got out of bed. She went to the living room, turned on all the lamps and walked around. "Oh mama," she said to herself. She looked toward the chained and bolted front door and then onto the enclosed porch, where photos lay in piles among packing boxes. Somehow the sight of the old photographs steadied her. She turned out the lights and returned to her bedroom. But even more than before, she felt the presence of someone else in the room. And in some recess of her mind, as she crawled back under the covers, she heard Mary's carefree girl giggling, and then her mature but ever-young laughter. She almost felt a playful hug. "Curious," she thought.

But also scary.

She quickly tuned in the radio to Starlight's frequency, and when she reclined back onto her pillows she kept the lamp on. Under the circumstances, it was actually comforting to hear the voice of Joan, the alien abductee. Jack Kestle had brought her on again by popular demand. She was saying the same thing that the psychic Thomas Van Dorn had said, that we're each a bunch of different selves, sharing a body like some kind of rooming house.

"Doesn't that seem awfully fragmented?" Jack asked.

"Not if you consider the ultimate unity of all consciousness," Joan replied cheerfully.

"Okay," Jack conceded reluctantly, "I'll grant that."

One thing a lot of listeners were concerned with, Jack went on, was the question of whether Joan's experience with the inter-dimensional being had been voluntary. "I've gotten quite a number of e-mails," he said. "And to be blunt, I guess the concern is that, well, given the fact that you were abducted, that this could be seen as a rape."

"I can see why some would think that," Joan said calmly. "But you have to realize, Jack, that once I was in this other realm, I felt perfectly comfortable. This being and I established an immediate rapport."

"I see, so you weren't . . ."

"I wasn't unwilling, if that's what you're asking."

"I know we've been through this before," Jack said, "and supposedly this whole visual thing is a male hang-up. But still, it's hard to believe that you could look at this reptilian being—I have a sketch here everybody, and it's sort of a cross between a Komodo dragon and a crocodile—and be turned on."

"I can see why you would say that, Jack. But at first this being appeared as a very handsome earth male—sort of a cross between Leonard DiCaprio and Tom Cruise."

"Whoa, wait a minute! This is something new. You didn't tell us that before. And when did he reveal himself as he actually is?"

"While we were . . . well . . . in the act, I guess you'd say."

"Wait a minute. Didn't that freak you out?"

"Not at all. I should probably add that these beings are capable of endless shapeshifting. Who knows what his actual self is, whatever that means on his plane of reality? He may simply have appeared in a way that I projected."

"But why on earth would you project Komodo-man?"

"Isn't it obvious?" Joan said. "It's because I was psychically prepared to reactivate that deeply buried soul memory, so that I could continue my journey and do what I have to do here, in this lifetime."

"The shaft of light thing and all that?"

"That's right."

Peg turned off the light. After lowering the volume on the radio, she lay in the dark and allowed a quiet reality to settle in around her. She was feeling edgy about the voice she had heard coming through the radio static, but she also felt a precipitant energy, an energy which seemed to beckon her toward some new and vital experience. She turned again toward the radio and turned up the volume. Placing a crooked finger on the tuning knob, she rotated it delicately away from Starlight's frequency until the funny staticky sounds came. Then she lay back on her pillows and waited, picturing a deep, dark and endless sky in her mind.

She must have dozed off, because the words broke in on her awareness as if through a viscous bubble. "I'm okay," the voice said. Then static. "We're all okay." More static. And finally, "It's not your fault." Peg sat bolt upright in the bed. She wasn't afraid, just focused, intent, and receptive to the utmost of her capacities. She waited and listened, but no more came. It was just funny radio sounds. She lay back on her pillows and fell soundly asleep.

In the morning she again felt the funny presence of Mary around her, sensed the carefree girlish laughter of the days before her sister became troubled and moody. She was acutely aware of all kinds of sounds she never normally noticed, like the ticking of the clock, the hum of the radio when it was switched off, or air breathing from the ducts in the walls. The singing and whining of the pipes while she took her shower seemed to be saying something, but she had no desire to try and make it out.

While she was dressing, she glimpsed Richard's letter sitting unanswered on the bureau. She took up a pen and a note card and without really thinking jotted a brief note. "I'm okay," she wrote. "We're all okay. It's not your fault."

Bud came by that evening to pick her up for dinner. He was still trying to make up for his earlier gaffe.

"You been listening to that Starlight Radio lately?" he asked brightly, as if it were one of his favorites.

"Not really," she said.

She began to sleep better. One night she fell into a profound slumber while picturing the deep and starry sky. She was gently awakened by music that sounded like running your finger around the wet edge of a wine glass. She sat up in bed as a shaft of the purest white light engulfed her room. "I hope it's not the lizard one," she thought. Then there was a sort of whoosh, and she found herself on a blue sphere floating through radiant space.

All at once came flooding into her mind all the people she had ever known and loved, like the photographs on the bulletin boards and in the boxes on the porch. Only they weren't mere pictures, but more like fragments of herself, alive and reaching out to her and to one another, a stream of life with no beginning and no end. Her mother and father, and Mary, and her brother Ralph came into focus, and she heard their words in her mind. "We're okay." Her daughter, sons and the "little sweeties" were also there somehow, and she saw them as they were, struggling with their lives here on earth. She saw Bud and all of her friends both living and dead, and she saw Richard in his Florida golf home relaxing, and she felt happy for him and peaceful.

Suddenly there was like a zap, and she was back in her room and the day was dawning. She got up and dressed, and then she set right to work on her sifting and sorting. She felt that she would have to work steadily, but somehow she knew that there would be enough time to care for everything as she ought to.

In the mid-morning Dexter called to check on her.

"Anything new, Ma?" he asked.

"No, nothing new. Just sorting and sifting. It's an endless task, you know."

He on Honeydew Hath Fed

And all should cry, Beware! Beware!
His flashing eyes, his floating hair!
Weave a circle round him thrice,
And close your eyes with holy dread,
For he on honey-dew hath fed,
And drunk the milk of Paradise . . .
Coleridge, *Kubla Khan*

I'VE KNOWN ROBERT since the third grade. We met in the shy way of eight-year-olds, outside the reddish trailer that served as our classroom that awful autumn that Kennedy was shot. I still remember being sent home after the principal came over the loudspeaker and Mrs. Allgood, whose stone-gray hair was slashed by a triangular blaze of white above her forehead, spoke to the children of our class in muted, gentle tones. I also happen to remember (I have an odd penchant for remembering even the smallest details) Robert's short essay about the assassination, which starkly enumerated the events surrounding the shooting in simple, chronological sequence.

We lost track of one another until the sixth grade again brought us into the same classroom. We were all developing our social identities that year, and our "crowd" formed bonds with the crazy energy of sub-atomic particles. Robert and I were inseparable until we took up different interests in high school, he in rock n' roll, I in the students at a nearby Catholic girls school. We remained buddies, of course, but our orbits intersected less frequently.

There came another cycle of separation when my parents moved to California at the time I went off to college. During the long years working on my doctorate Robert and I saw each other infrequently, and after I took a teaching job in Wisconsin, years passed without any communication between us. Through an extraordinary set of circumstances I won't go into (that's an altogether different story) we have come back into contact recently, and another cycle of friendship has given us both, I like to think, an anchor to our pasts.

'Pierre, you showed up just in time,' he said recently, reviving an old habit of referring to one another by monikers from Mademoiselle Turner's eighth-grade French class.

My friend was approaching what Lawrence Durrell's *Justine* protagonist called the "dead level of things." His wife had left him after a decade of marriage; and this dislocation, and the wounded feelings which accompanied it, had sent him scrambling not so much for cover—although that was, understandably, his first impulse—as for some key to unlock the mysteries of human life and fate.

He had already been through many incarnations, as if he were trying to live a multitude of lives in one lifespan. He had been a popular leader during our school years until, falling in with the counterculture, he eschewed all attachment to anything sanctioned by the "establishment." That was when he took to playing guitar in rock n' roll bands, grew his hair long, and made a point of wearing shabby clothes. None of it, at the time, made much sense to me. I was brought up on classical music, and while I enjoyed the weekly teen dances as much as anyone—they afforded plentiful opportunities to "make out"—and gladly sang along with the insubstantial tunes that came over the radio when we cruised with friends, I couldn't imagine what drove someone with Robert's intelligence to devote the better part of his free time to the production of what struck me as amateurish noise. What was he after? I couldn't make it out. As for the counterculture, I have never felt the need to rebel against the "system," though I was okay with the free love part. I have always had my own ways of getting what I wanted.

Normally by stealth.

I don't mean to say that Robert and I could no longer talk, quite the contrary. We continued to share a lot of common ground, and aside from the favors one expects of a buddy—I like to remember it was in my car, borrowed for the occasion, that he got his first lay—we frequently sat late into the night, sustaining ourselves with sandwiches made by pressing a couple slices of American cheese between two pieces of toast (a sort of poor man's grilled cheese) and with the kinds of discussions typical of adolescents confronting the multifarious options of adult life. Kurt Vonnegut was big then, and transactional analysis (I'm O.K., You're O.K.?) along with a host of other "new" ideas, and Robert frequently brought our discussions around to such utopian conceptions then making the rounds as pacifism, free love, and communal living.

The war in 'Nam was winding down, but Nixon was still bombing the North, not to mention Cambodia and Laos, and Robert was deeply affected by the violence going on over there. In this I thought him a bit emotional, and perhaps even subject to manipulation by an overtly anti-war press. The famous photograph of the girl with napalm burns, running along a road, for example, made a great impression on him; in fact, it seemed to settle, without need for further criteria, his views on the subject. He was sympathetic to communism then, a view I didn't share, and one he himself has since relinquished.

But neither of us were happy with the prix fixe menu offered by American society, which as far as we both could determine consisted of working your brains out until you collapse on the operating table, with TV as your only consolation along the way. If I have been less rebellious it is because, as I have said, I early on learned to get what I want—leaving aside whether it's what I *should* want—without making an open break with the system. In fact, I have found that the "system" affords me a certain shelter which I find reassuring, and a cover of sorts. I have played the tweedy academic to the hilt, and while I have not lost my fascination with the great minds, I'm just as fascinated with the great legs of the co-eds they send into my classrooms every semester.

But enough on me; it's my old friend Robert I'm trying to describe here. As I said, he went through many incarnations. He gave up the idea of becoming a rock n' roll musician (thank God!) when he went off to college, where he buried himself in his studies, favoring literature, history, and cultural anthropology. The energy that had propelled him to lead so many extra-curricular activities during our school years now took an inward turn, and he became the soul of the *vita contemplativa*, as before he had been an exemplar of the *vita activa*. He was never without a book in these years, and when we caught up with one another around holidays or over summer vacation, we found that our conversations, so inchoate and unstructured when we were in high school, took on a more pointed character, our serious studies having provided us with a satchelful of shiny, sharp instruments with which to dissect life.

Unable to settle on a major, Robert wound up with a degree in general humanities. This was a classic Robertian move: refusing to allow himself to be pinned down, to become a settled quantity. After a couple of false starts in graduate programs he took a try at law school, but this only ended by filling him with disgust—mainly at himself, I believe, for attempting something so alien to his nature.

It was at this point that Robert and I began to lose touch with one another, not on account of any plan, certainly, but due rather to a combination of dumb luck and the inattentiveness of youth. I was already fixed in my path, following the advanced studies in philosophy, with a special emphasis on scientific materialism, that would make my career. Looking back now, I realize that I was living in a tunnel, unable to see much beyond the very small and distant light at its end. Of course I allowed myself the occasional distraction. . . .

I had infrequent news of Robert, sometimes through a mutual friend or, more rarely, when I found myself back in Washington, where I still had family. Based on these scant gleanings, I developed the impression that, cut loose from the moorings of college and university, he had allowed his protean nature to run rampant. He studied anything and everything, from ancient Greece, to economics, to physics. He hotly debated politics, as he was still attached to the idea of some utopian solution for humanity. His tendency towards nature worship, which had always existed in embryo, and to which his studies of Wordsworth and Emerson now provided a philosophical undergirding, intensified; he frequently went off on solitary hikes in the Shenandoah Mountains. While retaining the bookish attractions he had developed in college, he passed through a series of fascinations with such popular art forms as jazz, foreign art cinema, and modern novels. He seemed particularly attracted to those excrescence's of culture that took him away from the familiar and the safe, or those which suggested other worlds; it was as though he felt a need to be reminded of some continually shifting horizon, moving always toward an unattainable distance. I remember his particular fascination with some Brazilian singer—Gilberto was the name, I believe—whose bossa nova music he invested with the sort of religious significance I reserve for Bach's *B Minor Mass* or *Mahler's 9th*. On one of my rare visits he took me to see a Spanish art film with no dialogue, one he had seen several times, consisting entirely of the rehearsal of a flamenco dance troop for an upcoming performance. I found it interesting, but I failed to understand the state of rapture to which it transported my friend. While I sought an anchor in the solid traditions of logical thought, Robert was content to sail upon an endless sea of exploration, with no terminus to his voyage, no port of debarkation . . .

He worked at a series of jobs, none with any future. Despite recurring bouts of anxiety over his career, I believe he was incapable of resisting the urge, now an habitual reflex with him, to explore the various potentialities of man, and of his own being, as free as possible from other obligations.

Those of us who knew him wondered where it would all end. While we settled more or less comfortably into our niches in society, he seemed determined to accept nothing less than a complete and total understanding of the human experience—a Faustian endeavor, to be sure. To revive my nautical metaphor, no safe harbor interested him. It's as if he were trying to transcend himself, to be something bigger, more encompassing, to be, perhaps . . . everything!

Did I feel sorry for my friend during those years? He staked his life on the most slender of reeds—art, literature, history, and other abstractions—at the cost of the concrete compensations that, for most of us, make life bearable. Eschewing the established ways of society, he pursued his course with what was, after all, a reckless faith in his own inner compass, his own subjective promptings. And didn't this amount to nothing more than a ridiculous faith in human nature itself?

As we completely lost touch over the following years, Robert appears to have followed this strain to its logical conclusions. I know now that he became enamored of the works of Carlos Castaneda—that clever fraud—delved into the practice of shamanism, and got involved with yogic meditation. Marriage must have added some stability to his life, and he fell into a little business which enabled him enough income to support a modest lifestyle. Of chief concern to Robert, the enterprise's irregular commitments afforded him plenty of free time for the study and exploration without which he could not live.

When we came together again, after many years, I was curious to see what had become of my old friend. I was more or less enjoying life, though I had no illusions that my philosophy classes were changing the world. The intricacies of formal thought still fascinated me, and the academy offered a refuge from the crassness of society. I occasionally experienced what might even be called a spiritual connection with my students.

As I have noted, I found Robert confronting that "dead level" of things. Along with the more obvious hardships following on the departure of his wife, he was experiencing a crisis of confidence, one no doubt occasioned by that critical blow to his solar plexus. He had begun to question his lifelong program, his quest for knowledge, experience, and self-awareness, and even to wonder if the entire endeavor had not been a colossal failure. He had always assumed that if he followed his impulses, his intuition, everything would turn out well. He had taken for granted that he would discover some grand principle, or produce some great gift for humanity: perhaps the gift of the cultivation of the human spirit and, with that, the perfect freedom he sought. But now his faith was shaken. He was approaching forty with no wife or family, and no role in society remotely commensurate with the abilities that his friends had always recognized. He had taken to writing poetry and stories but had yet to come up with anything he felt comfortable publishing. Some of it was quite decent, but his efforts invariably failed to live up to his impossibly high standards. He wanted masterpieces or nothing. As always, it was some abstract absolute that seemed to interest him, rather than just "getting along."

"Man's reach must exceed his grasp," he was fond of quoting.

Finding Robert in this condition was troubling for

me. We never doubted him in our school days, when his confidence was prodigious. He knew the answer to every question, the egress from every dilemma. No, I have never known anyone as natural and free of misgivings as Robert was then. He was the guy who always explained our situation to teachers, parents, and even to ourselves. Later, when our interests diverged, I watched from a distance, with a combination of fear and awe, as he carried on his tightrope walk through life, determined to discover upon how slender a base of security he could pursue his enthusiasms . . .

Now he was humbled. But perhaps he wasn't beaten. He had reached a point where he had little left to lose, yet he was determined to find anything of value left to him, and to hold on to that vestige come hell or high water. He examined every aspect of his life, trying to figure out what had gone wrong, and how he could do better. If life was a staring match of the kind we used to amuse ourselves with as schoolboys, he was determined not to be the first one to blink.

Our rapport when I returned to Washington, in spite of the years of separation, was completely natural; and our friendship effortlessly took up the rhythm of our school days. I'd ring him on a Saturday morning and say, "Whadda ya wanna do today?" feeling like I was fourteen again. "Should I come over to your place, or do you wanna come over here?" We would laugh about how little things had changed.

In between tennis or chess matches, movies or restaurant dinners, I would steer the conversation around to Robert's personal situation. I was concerned about him, and I felt obliged to keep tabs on how he was faring.

Our conversations often returned to a voyage Robert had made to India a couple of years earlier. I will relate that journey in some detail, since Robert places such emphasis on certain experiences he had over its course. The story intrigues me, I suppose, because it goes to the heart of the yin and yang that has always formed a pleasant dichotomy in our relationship. As you will see, he attaches considerable, perhaps supreme, importance to certain inner experiences, data which I cannot help but examine in an objective light.

I will nonetheless present Robert's story—as far as is humanly possible—from his point of view, leaving aside my own objections until I am finished. He has related the tale to me on several occasions and I, fascinated not only with the window it provides into the workings of my friend's psyche but also the ontological questions it so clearly raises, have questioned him in detail on various points. These details are now stored in that blasted memory of mine, and on one level I write, I suppose, for no other reason than to attempt to expunge them.

I am no writer; that is my old friend's bag, not mine. So I hope you will forgive me if I miss some of the obvious narrative devices (tricks, you might say) or even if what is called the "point-of-view" isn't what one of my colleagues in the literature department might prefer. You see, as often as I've heard it, and with Robert and I being such old friends, I feel that his story has become mine as well. So I intend to relate it in simple fashion, quoting his words when it seems appropriate, but always presenting the account along the lines he presented it to me.

&&&

Robert journeyed to India with his then wife, Gretchen, and an older man of Indian provenance whom she called her guru. *GuruJi*, as Gretchen referred to the man (adding the fond suffix employed by the guru's followers) ran a retreat center in the Pennsylvania countryside, some hundred miles from Washington. Gretchen traveled there regularly with the friend and colleague who introduced her to the guru. (Being a musician, a classical cellist, her work life allowed her the flexibility to devote each Tuesday to the Center's weekly meditation workshop, normally followed by a private consultation with GuruJi himself.)

The guru's meditation system was grounded in the chanting of *mantras*: short devotional hymns, directed to one or another of the various gods of the Hindu pantheon, voiced in the ancient holy tongue of Sanskrit. A novitiate's personal mantra would be chanted quietly for brief intervals during mediation; in the interstices which followed, the aspirant would sit silently with breath steady, absorbing the special energies it was thought that the mantra had called forth. To have a personal mantra was to have a special talisman, a vehicle which might carry one to liberation from the egoistic desires which, according to the tenets of all great world religions, engender so much human anguish. A key of such power and promise, understandably, was not easily acquired. Indeed, a mantra was to be had for neither love nor money, but could be received only at the hands of a being far advanced upon the journey to soul liberation.

Gretchen's guru was considered by his followers to be just such a being; and it was he who, after private consultation with the aspirant, would assign a specific mantra, tailored to the student's needs, to be used in daily mediation. Sitting before the student, he would himself demonstrate how to chant the mantra in his remarkably nuanced voice, capable of all manner of quarter-tones and dynamic contrasts, with variations in tone from sweet clarity to nasal whines or guttural rumbles. During subsequent consultations, the student would chant the mantra back to the guru, so that he might gauge her progress. As the student advanced in the guru's eyes, he might assign new, additional mantras. His more accomplished students possessed several. A mantra was a precious, and sacred, possession. Once assigned one, the student was not to share this information with others, nor would she ever voice the hymn outside the sacred space of meditation. The mantra was not just another song; it was a psychic tool of special power.

During the weekly meditation classes, and at seasonal five-day retreats, the guru would sit upon a raised dais at the head of the meditation room and break forth, one after another, in unearthly renderings of the entire range of mantras which made up his vast repertoire. In between these bursts of sound the class would sit in silent meditation, absorbing the effects produced upon the limbic system and other neural centers by his wild vocalizations. The classes, in this sense, represented a version, writ large, of the mediation practices taught by the guru; profiting no less from the guru's extraordinary vocal abilities than his intimate knowledge of the mantra system, the students could experience the full power of these ancient syllables when employed to their richest effect. Robert, who had on occasion attended these classes, was effusive in his descriptions.

Isolated in the silence of the old farmstead where the retreat center was located, sitting cross-legged upon cushions with the other students and primed by a day of fasting, Robert experienced the guru's impassioned vocal onslaughts (with their "exotic eastern scales and microtones, their droning lows, or soaring flights to whinging trebles") as a "veritable body blow."

The guru believed that sounds, and more specifically the sacred sounds of mantras, burnished over thousands of years by dedicated Hindu psychonauts, possessed the capacity to operate directly upon the Chakra system of the listener. In the guru's world, blockages in the various Chakras—those seven ethereal centers ascending from the base of the coccyx to the top of the head, conceived in Hindu philosophy as the loci of our physical, emotional, and spiritual lives—were responsible for our inability to experience the bliss of true liberation. When the guru met with a student in private consultation, based on what was accepted as the extraordinary intuitive powers of a "higher being," he would assign a personal mantra designed to erode those Chakra blockages (be they in the Heart Chakra, responsible for feeling, or the Wind Chakra, responsible for personal expression) which he determined constituted the most grievous barriers to the student's progress toward spiritual freedom. Exposure to the guru's expert chanting during classes and retreats, covering the entire range of mantras, was seen as a sort of all-Chakra tune-up, and was thought to benefit everyone present.

There were many further complications to the guru's system, for those who followed it fully. The guru believed, for example, that astronomical events affect our psyches through the principles of astrology, the history of which is ancient on the Indian subcontinent. For this reason his more dedicated students practiced breathing exercises keyed to phases of the moon; they even based their daily wardrobe choices on colors associated with each day's ruling celestial power—such as silver for "Moon" day, gold for "Sun" day, or red for "Tues" day (the day named in English for the Norse god of war, ever associated with the red planet Mars, an association more explicit in the French *mardi* or the Spanish *martes*). There were also devotional statues, assigned by the guru, like the mantras, only after careful consideration of the students' worthiness; *yantras*, geometric representations of metaphysical reality akin to the Buddhist *mandalas* the hippy types all had on their dorm walls in college; various dietary restrictions and regular fasts; specially tailored yoga postures; and much more.

In submitting herself to the guru's tutelage, Robert's ex-wife Gretchen found a path that spoke to all of her deepest strivings in life. I suppose we should not find it surprising that a professional musician would be drawn to a spiritual practice centered on sound; a woman who, as Robert told me, could be delivered to rapturous states by Bach and Rachmaninoff was obviously a woman deeply sensitive to the potent effects of aural vibrations on the human psyche. And as we have indicated, the guru was a consummate virtuoso in his chosen form: the Hindu, or Vedic, mantra. But a mere susceptibility to music could not explain the depth of Gretchen's dedication to the guru's system, a dedication which went far beyond a fascination with mantra chanting. She in fact bought into the entire gamut of spiritual practices the Indian recommended. She missed the Center's weekly classes only for the most compelling of reasons, and she conducted her pre-dawn mediations with a rigorous regularity, stuffing one or the other of her nostrils with cotton in order to adjust her breathing to the phases of the moon. She kept a daily diary in which she documented her attempts to curtail those ploys of the sneaky ego to direct her life, and two or three gaudily painted statuettes—idols, if we are to be honest—lived on the small table before which she practiced her daily rites. Her diet consisted chiefly of vegetarian curries, and she even took to wearing cotton kurta pajamas, the everyday garment of traditional India, on a regular basis.

She developed a deep devotion to the guru.

Gretchen also developed a strong attachment to the guru's assistant, a Dutch woman whose name was Johanna but whom Robert often referred to as "the Enforcer." As the guru was considered a "highly evolved being," a strict system of protocol governed his interactions with the Center's meditation students. After concluding his weekly chanting sessions in the converted farmhouse's large living room, he would step immediately away from the dais and whisk himself into the hallway, his flowing robes trailing his long frame, and up the steps to his private quarters on the second floor. The students were never to engage him in casual conversation. They only spoke with him during private consultations, for which, I should add, they paid a healthy fee.

Given the guru's inaccessibility, it was to Johanna that Gretchen and her fellow mediation students turned with the manifold problems they encountered in following the guru's difficult regimens: to go over their daily ego diaries or to perfect their mantras, to learn how to make special curries, schedule attendance at classes and retreats, or to make appointments with the guru. Johanna stood as a barrier between the students and the master, interpreting and clarifying his instructions while also protecting him from the unwanted attentions of what could be considered, if we wish to be uncharitable, spiritual groupies. In her late forties or early fifties by Robert's estimation, unmarried, Johanna was a pleasant-looking woman whom Robert characterized as mild-mannered on the surface but capable of Machiavellian coldheartedness when the guru's interests, or those of the spiritual protocols which were her life's purpose, were at stake. She had followed the guru for many years and, unlike the guru himself, who lived in town with his wife and teenaged sons, dwelled in the farmhouse at the mediation center. Having practiced the guru's regimens for many years, and enjoying his complete confidence, she was considered by the Center's students to be far advanced along the road to liberation, though naturally not in the same class as the guru himself.

"If the guru was the general," Robert told me, "Johanna was the major."

In Robert's estimation, the assistant came to be something of a surrogate mother for his wife, just as he believed that Gretchen's attachment to the guru was an attempt to gain a father more suitable than the one whom fate had handed her. A career army sergeant who met and married Gretchen's mother while stationed in Germany during the American occupation, a wartime injury which frustrated his dreams to become a professional violinist rendered him an embittered and angry drunkard who committed acts against his children with which I will not sully this account. Gretchen had been spared the most heinous crimes, but she had been too often pummeled and, though of a forgiving nature, she could not look upon the man who committed these and even worse outrages against her siblings as a parent. Though Gretchen was close to her mother, the fact that for so many years she failed to shield her children from such horrors—even if she claimed not to have known the worst of it—must have, in Robert's view, created an equal longing in Gretchen for a mother figure in whom she could place her total confidence.

The guru and his assistant, by Robert's account, made the perfect surrogate parents. The guru, like the traditional father, was the ultimate source of all blessings. Remote and placid, he was not to be bothered about trivial matters. His demeanor was gentle, but his pronouncements were accepted as divine and unquestionable truth. It was the assistant who, like the dutiful mother, got into the trenches with the students, confronting the myriad day-to-day problems involved in seeking self-mastery. When they complained of the rigors of the guru's system, she would remind them of their inner saboteurs, of the frightful tenacity of our petty egos to rule our lives, making us and everyone around us miserable in the process.

Robert did not share Gretchen's attachment to the guru or to his assistant Johanna, and when he spoke of the rivalries and jealousies among the guru's mainly female followers (which seem inevitable in such settings) it was with a wry detachment. Nor did he take to the entirety of the guru's elaborate program for spiritual advancement. He was, nonetheless, a committed believer in the salutary effects of pre-dawn meditations, accompanied by the chanting of mantra, which he himself took up after visiting the retreat center a year after Gretchen began to attend its classes. If not a professional musician like Gretchen, he was nonetheless an enthusiastic amateur, also highly sensitive to Orpheus's charms (it was while watching Gretchen perform Bach's unaccompanied cello suite at a downtown church one quiet Sunday afternoon, he once told me, that he decided that he would marry her). He had met in private consultation with the guru and received from him a couple of rudimentary mantras to use in his daily rites. He had also accompanied Gretchen to the classes on several occasions, and he even participated in one of the Center's five-day-long cleansing retreats, a biannual fillip marked by intestinal purging and a near continual barrage of heady mantra chanting by the guru. Robert credited his involvement with the guru's system with helping him to clarify his life and purposes; nor can it be said, Robert being a committed vegetarian, that he had any complaints about the increasingly fine curries Gretchen brought forth from the kitchen of the cramped, World War II – era apartment they shared on the edge of the city.

The high-water mark of the mediation center's annual calendar was an event billed as "Journey to the Source." Each summer the guru traveled back to India to visit a man he considered to be his own spiritual guide, a reclusive swami and disciple of the late Hindu saint Ramana Maharshi. For a fee that I judged neither obscene nor inconsequential, students at the mediation center could accompany the guru on this journey—to the "source," as it were. After accomplishing the Journey two times on her own,

Gretchen began, a couple of years prior to their separation, to encourage Robert to accompany her. He was, it must be said, in no way immune to her blandishments. I remember his fascination with the very thought of India, when he first read of its swamis and sages as a college student (I still picture the photograph of loincloth-clad devotees, hoisting the elephant-headed god above the dusk-lit waters of a dark lagoon, which in those days occupied a place on his desk.)

The guru had himself, during one of Robert's infrequent private consultations, encouraged Robert to make the "journey."

"Just think," the guru told him in the casual, lolling way he adopted when he addressed his followers in private, his rich brown eyes shining softly, "a few days of *darshan* with SwamiJi is worth several lifetimes of *sadhana.*"[1]

Robert joked to Gretchen and her friends from the meditation center that the trip was indeed a bargain, if two weeks of darshan visits could absolve him of a lifetime of the guru's mediation practice—a practice which required him to rise an hour before sunrise each day of the year.

"I figure I can quit doing sadhana for a couple of lifetimes now," he quipped, invoking an "Oh. . . ." from Gretchen—an "oh" that conveyed an appreciation of his sense of humor, along with a too-tender faith that he couldn't possibly be serious about abandoning the spiritual practice that had come to occupy the core of her existence.

Robert had no intention, in fact, of renouncing his daily meditations. Though he did not follow the entire complicated array of the guru's practices, as I have written, he had

1 *Darshan* is a Sanskrit term indicating an audience with a holy man; *sadhana* refers to the daily practice of meditation and mantra chanting in which the guru instructed his charges.

deposited no small amount of hope in mantra meditation as the avenue by which he might discover the ultimate sense of completion he sought, an awareness of all and that all is well, that the world in its continual permutations actually made sense, that it is a place where he could feel comfortable and at home—*bon dans son peau*, as the French like to say. Though he joked about the guru's remarks, having heard my friend's tale, I can say that the guru's promise of a sumptuous spiritual harvest to be had at the feet of the distant swami was not without its effect upon his decision to join the group on their journey.

Nor, in the sequel, was that promise disappointed.

During Robert's last private consultation, the guru, purportedly employing that capacity to look deeply into the essential nature of others with which his followers credited him, had said, "You will always seek the highest source of truth." And when Robert looked back upon his journey to India, describing it to me, he seemed to conceive of his darshans with the swami in precisely that vein. The guru himself, after all, considered the swami to be well above his own station on the spiritual ladder; to be, in fact, the *non plus ultra* of Indian wisdom. "To continue the metaphor," Robert had told me, "if the guru was the general, and the Enforcer the major, the swami was the Field Marshal."

Robert's visits to the swami's hut in fact marked the beginning of the end of his involvement with Gretchen's guru and the guru's meditation center. As Robert described it to me, the swami did not practice the involved system of ritual acts propounded by Gretchen's guru, but instead followed a path of relentless self-inquiry propounded by his teacher, Ramana Maharshi, whose spiritual quest began and ended with the simple question, "Who am I?" The swami's intellectually rigorous discourses on the three states of human consciousness—waking, sleeping, and dreaming—not only challenged all of Robert's conceptions about life, they convinced him that the swami had seen into the very heart of human experience. The message Robert carried away from his encounters with the swami was that his ultimate liberation, should it be achieved, would come as a result of an unfettered soul searching, rather than the slavish adherence to meticulously chanted prayers, idol worship, ritual fasting, and observance of the phases of the moon advocated by Gretchen's guru.

Robert's separation from the guru and his center was hastened along by several striking incidents, both pleasant and unpleasant, which occurred during his journey. These episodes constitute an odd mélange of personal rivalries and intrigue, interspersed with occurrences of capital import to which my friend ascribes supernatural implications (his claim, for example, that he, and Gretchen along with him, witnessed a stone statue of the god Shiva physically breathing at the Elephanta caves off the coast at Mumbai!). Along with the profound influence of the saintly swami, these events conspired to show Robert other paths to the spiritual fulfillment he sought, both more comprehensive and more congenial to Robert's essential nature than that advocated by Gretchen's guru.

&&&

Robert and Gretchen flew into Bangalore, via Mumbai, where they connected with the rest of the guru's group.

There were, along with Robert and Gretchen, a couple from New Jersey named Ward and Linda; two sisters from Connecticut; Jenni, a Danish therapist; and the dour Dutch businessman Heinz. Neither the guru himself nor his assistant were with them; they had traveled to India the week before. After a day's stay in what Robert called "that thriving, ramshackle megalopolis," they made a harrowing, eight-hour journey by minibus to the ancient city of Mysore.

"If you've ever seen chicken played with moving automobiles at sixty miles per hour," Robert recounted to me, "it isn't pretty. Heinz, in his deadpan, Flemish way, finally said to the driver, 'It's more important than we get to Mysore *alive* than that we get there *quickly*.'"

In Mysore, "with its wide ceremonial plaza and shabbily grand palace," the group put up in a small hotel on the city's outskirts called—suspiciously, I thought—the "Darshan Suites," where the guru and his assistant awaited them. The reclusive swami they had come to attend lived in a concrete hut ("no larger than a garden shed") amid the fields of a patron's coconut plantation in the surrounding countryside. The guru had arranged for his meditation students to have darshan with the holy man nearly every day of their stay in Mysore.

In the pre-dawn twilight the students would gather on the rooftop of the hotel, a four-story structure, for morning meditations (Robert: "the sound of calling koyals and chanting priests rising from the misty landscape below"). These sessions, featuring the usual mantra chanting, interspersed with silent sitting, would be supervised by the assistant. Later in the morning, the students were instructed in the singing of Vedic hymns by two Indian musicians the guru had contracted for that purpose.

Each afternoon the meditation students boarded three auto rickshaws that stood waiting by pre-arrangement in front of the hotel. The guru and his assistant would not be with them for, having spent the morning with the swami, they awaited them in the countryside. Instead the students were accompanied by the guru's middle-aged sister, Anjali, whom the guru had arranged to handle the material needs of his students while they were in India. A cheerful, caring sort ("lovely, in a matronly way," Robert said, "with her dark, flowing hair, her colorful saris enwrapping a slight plumpness that bespoke a simple ease in the world"), she accompanied them to meals in the local curry houses, carefully making sure that everyone got enough to eat; saw to it that the *dhobi*[2] took care of their laundry; quarreled with peddlers for better prices; admonished rickshaw drivers; and took care of other practical matters deemed outside the spiritual functions not only of the guru, but also of his assistant.

With Anjali as their guide, the pilgrims rumbled over the uneven macadam road that led from Mysore into the countryside, past the wall where old ladies plastered cow dung to dry for fuel, past a ragtag general store and up the hill that taxed the weak motors of the rickshaws to the utmost. Not long after clearing the crest of the hill, a half-hour after leaving the hotel, they would reach the dirt lane leading to the swami's concrete hut, which in the parlance of the guru's tradition was referred to as a *kutiya*—that is,

---

2 The *dhobi* caste of India discharges the occupation of clothes washing.

the dwelling place of a renunciate. This lane was lined with the low-slung houses of peasants who worked on the plantation; as the rickshaws sputtered along, turning up clouds of dust, villagers would line the lane to greet the fare-skinned aliens with the pressed-hands gesture known as *pranam*, a gesture invariably returned by the rickshaws' passengers, delighted, as they were, by the simple, welcoming friendliness of these humble people.

A great fuss was made over protocol for visiting the swami. The guru, as has been noted, considered the man a being even more highly evolved than himself: one who over the course of manifold reincarnations had purified his eternal soul to an uncommon extent, burning off the dross of egoism and sensual desire that in Vedic philosophy together keep us mired, across an endless cycle of deaths and subsequent rebirths, in the tragic condition of being human. Because he followed a regimen of the strictest asceticism, the swami was said to be highly sensitive to stimuli of all kinds, a stimulation the avoidance of which was incidentally crucial to his continuing progress along the path of non-desire. For this reason the guru's charges were enjoined against wearing scents, forbidden to consume garlic or onions, instructed to shower prior to darshan, and asked to wear only white clothing to these visits. Instructions of this kind were invariably conveyed at the close of the pre-dawn mediation sessions by Johanna, the "Enforcer."

Roger had been looking forward to wearing the loose fitting white kurta pajamas he imagined to be common in India. He only spoke of the practical advantages of such a cool and yielding garment, but I believe that he also expected some more essential liberation, as if the donning of different clothing might magically turn him into a Gandhi. He already owned one set which Gretchen had bought for him on one of her previous trips to India. He planned to buy others in Mysore, but upon arriving there he discovered nothing in the shops but the cheap Western-style clothing now universally worn by Indian men.

After a couple days of darshan in Mysore's tropical heat Robert's single kurta set needed washing; he turned it over to the dhobi, which left him without white clothes for the next day's session. Gretchen offered to loan him one of her kurta pajamas and, as the man and wife were roughly the same size, fit was not a problem. Robert was not happy with the frilly feminine embroidery that covered the top piece, but Gretchen dismissed his concerns in the pragmatic manner Robert claimed to be typical of her. "No one's going to notice," she said cursorily, further remarking that he was too sensitive to the opinions of others. "Gretchen's mother was a war bride," Robert added by way of commentary, "brought to the U.S. from Germany by her father. When she arrived in the United States, she had to cope with a culture about which an awful lot was foreign. What's worse, she carried the stigma being one of them—the Nazis—even though she was only a teenager during the war years." According to Robert's analysis, Gretchen's mother coped with these perplexities through a habit of active unconcern for the opinions of neighbors, school officials, and the generality of the small town where Gretchen's father was stationed at a nearby army base. Most pertinent to Robert's marriage, he claimed that she had passed these attitudes along to her daughter. Robert recalled the advice she used to give Gretchen prior to her chamber music performances, as a palliative to the stage fright that regularly plagued her on these occasions. "Just imagine the whole audience is sitting on the toilet," she would say in the musical voice which Gretchen shared, only without the German accent, and the pair would break up laughing.

So Robert wore the tunic, embroidery and all, though he felt vaguely emasculated as the auto rickshaws bumped and rattled past the cow dung wall and the general store, and then laboriously up the hill toward the remote dirt lane which led to the swami's kutiya.

On their first visit to the swami, several days earlier, the old man had pointed out, as he greeted the westerners in the clearing in front of his hut, the presence of three golden eagles soaring overhead. He claimed that this was an auspicious sign for the pilgrims, for it was a Sunday, Vishnu's day, and the golden eagle is a symbol of that god. But there were no eagles on this bright afternoon when Robert stood under the south India sky in a field of green, with coconut palms ranged across the horizon, wearing a ladies kurta pajama set. Yielding to Gretchen's point of view, he forcefully put aside his concern over the outfit, remaining alert to the signals of the Enforcer so that he might negotiate all of the involved protocols governing relations with the swami.

In addition to the proscriptions already mentioned, it was inappropriate, for example, to look into the swami's eyes (one might "drain" his energy); shoes, of course, were to be removed prior to entering the kutiya; and upon entering, it was proper to bend forward and touch the floor with one's fingertips, then touching these to the forehead. The swami was not to be addressed, once inside the hut, unless he addressed you first—every effort, in fact, was to be made to avoid drawing attention to yourself in any manner, for this would constitute an eruption of the ego, the quelling of which was the very purpose of the pilgrims' journey. Most importantly, under no circumstance should the least bodily contact be permitted to take place with the holy recluse.

This prohibition against bodily contact came into play especially at the end of the visits, after the swami had delivered his discourses on the states of consciousness, when he stood outside his hut and distributed *prasad* (sweets, or pieces of fruit, blessed with the potent energies believed to be at the disposal of an enlightened being). The Enforcer, sitting on the rooftop of the Darshan Suites Hotel, had graphically demonstrated the technique for receiving the prasad. The hands were to be cupped and held out passively, allowing the swami to drop the treat into them without making contact.

As the swami himself appeared to be completely unconcerned about the possibility of being touched, it could be difficult for the visitor to insure that this transgression did not occur. If he were to allow this to take place—or violate any of the other rules of protocol designed, as they were, to avoid impeding the swami's progress toward his imminent liberation—he was certain to incur the Hindu equivalent of fire and brimstone: "bad karma" (not to mention the active displeasure of the Enforcer).

The normal prasad was, quite naturally, a coconut. And on that day when Robert motor-rickshawed with the others to the swami's hut in a ladies kurta pajama, as the pilgrims filed out of the kutiya, misty with visions of transcendent reality, a couple of peasant boys appeared with their machetes, nicked and tarnished with use. A pile of fresh coconuts lay on the ground. Under the swami's direction, the boys went to work on the coconuts with their blades. After tapering the top down to a point, exposing the woody inner part of the shell, they would clip off the tip to create a hole through which a straw could be inserted to draw out the clear, mild milk. The swami would take each coconut as it was ready, insert a straw, and present it to one of his guests, who stood in a makeshift receiving line awaiting the prasads. After sipping out the milk, the visitor would return the hollow fruit to one of the machete-wielding youths, who would presently split the nut in two, generally with a single, deft stroke of his knife. The visitor could then eat the sweet, white flesh with a spoon he had brought along according to the Enforcer's instructions.

It was in the course of this highly ritualized procedure that occurred the first of those instances—we will refer to this episode as the *prasad incident*—which one by one eroded my friend's faith in the guru and his assistant, ultimately leading him to reconsider his involvement with the guru's meditation center.

The students stood beside one another in line, all in their white kurta pajamas, awaiting their prasads. Robert noticed that Gretchen stood at the end of the file and a little apart. There was a distracted air about her, he told me, as if something were wrong. She seemed drawn into herself, without the confident smile which typically graced her features. He could not perceive what events would soon prove: that she was coming down with something. It was mid-afternoon in India; no clouds shielded the tropical sun which bore down upon the little group of westerners standing in the wide clearing amid the coconut groves. The barefoot, robed swami was in the process of dropping a prepared coconut into the cupped hands of Linda—whom, for some reason, they all called Winky—when Robert heard a small sound which, as vague as it was, he recognized as coming from his wife. He and the others turned to see Gretchen falter, reach out her arms into the nothingness of air, stumble, and then drop heavily onto the dusty ground.

The students seemed uncertain what to do; the Enforcer had so impressed upon them the great delicacy surrounding every interaction with the swami that at first they stood frozen, waiting for some cue. After a moment Robert stepped discreetly over to where Gretchen lay, her eyes closed, and asked her what was the matter. "I started to feel faint," she said as she pulled herself up on one hip, supporting her weight with an outstretched arm. "I suddenly grew dizzy, and everything went white . . ."

The swami had deposited the coconut into Linda's hands and now moved over to where Gretchen sat. "Oh, my," he said as he crouched down and peered into her eyes. "What is the matter, my dear?" he asked kindly.

"I don't know," she replied quietly. "I just got dizzy . . . the sun . . . I don't know."

"Here, let me help you." The swami took Gretchen by the arm and helped her to stand. "Come over here into the shade," he said. "It will be cooler."

The swami said something in his language to one of the farm boys, who strode quickly off to the kutiya. He meanwhile directed Gretchen slowly toward the hut, Robert taking her other arm, and helped her to sit against its shaded wall. The farm boy now emerged from the hut with a couple of rags drenched in water and handed them to the swami. At this juncture, much to the surprise of the entire group, the swami knelt before Gretchen and began to apply these compresses to her feet! "This will make you feel better," he said.

Gretchen glanced—fretfully, Robert thought—toward Johanna. The Enforcer glared at her beneath her smile. Here was Gretchen breaking the most profound prohibition of interaction with the swami: bodily contact, and plenty of it! But what could she do? "I'm okay," she said, aware of the Enforcer's censorious stare, "I'll be fine." But the swami, oblivious to the meditation group's internecine dramas, and smiling benignly, continued his ministrations. "I'm very sorry," he said. "I should not have let you stand so long in the sun. You're probably not used to this heat. I hope you will be better soon."

Finally Johanna stepped up. "I think she's okay now, SwamiJi," she said flatly. "I'll take care of her."

The swami, mild as the madonna, was not one to dispute with the Enforcer. He slowly rose and went back to distributing his prasads, while Johanna knelt and spoke to Gretchen. "We'll talk about this later," she said. "Now why don't you see if you can stand up."

With help from Robert, Gretchen got back on her feet. She went to sit in one of the canopied auto-rickshaws, which had now appeared for the trip back to the hotel, while the others finished receiving their prasads.

There were no organized activities for the rest of the day, and while Robert and Gretchen relaxed in her room at the hotel (separate sleeping arrangements had been recommended for couples, to facilitate the "inner focus" which was the trip's stated purpose) the phone rang. It was

Johanna. Robert could tell from Gretchen's expression, suddenly sorrowful, that the conversation was not a pleasant one. In fact, Gretchen's periodic repetition of "Yes, Johanna," made it clear that she was receiving the Enforcer's version of a spiritual dressing-down. When she hung up the phone she burst into tears.

"She says I fainted on purpose," Gretchen sobbed, "just to get SwamiJi's attention!" She fell onto the bed.

"That's ridiculous," Robert rejoined. "You're jet-lagged, and we're all eating foods we're not used to. Sure, we've been careful to drink bottled water, but the restaurants wash their cutlery in tap water. Who knows what any of us might have been exposed to? Besides, it's probably a hundred degrees out there."

"But Johanna's right," Gretchen sniffled, sitting on the edge of the bed and gaining more possession of herself. "Deep inside, I do want SwamiJi's special attention. I would love nothing more than to be his favorite pupil, for him to place a hand on my head and zap me with *shaktipat*,[3] render me free from ego all at once!"

"Maybe we'd all like that," Robert countered, "but that doesn't mean we'd go around fainting just to get his attention. I'm sorry. Your willingness to examine yourself unsparingly is commendable, but I think Johanna's gone off on a tangent on this one. If you ask me, you either had heat exhaustion, or you're coming down with something."

"I don't know." She daubed at her nose with her kleenex.

---

3 *Shaktipat* refers to the process whereby it is believed that a highly evolved person may transmit spiritual enlightenment directly to another: by touch, sight, the bestowing of objects such as *prasad*, or even by thought alone.

"Johanna is just trying to help us evolve past our petty little emotional selves. I've got to rest. I think I'll lie down for a while."

Robert left her and went to walk among the narrow dirt lanes of the town, lined by the stalls of petty merchants and gaudy little shrines. He wanted to confront Johanna, tell her that she was wrong about Gretchen's motives, tell her even that he was surprised that she would bring his wife to tears for an instance of bodily weakness over which she had no control. But he thought better of it. He was not remotely as involved with the Center and its practices as was Gretchen, and he was reluctant to interfere in relationships and protocols about which there was much that he did not understand. Nor was his relationship with Gretchen based upon any tender protection of maid by man. Having come together as equals, they forged their own paths, she in her busy musical life, he in his many enthusiasms, meeting up at odd hours when their schedules conflated. "I had never fought her battles up to that point," he told me, "and it didn't seem natural to begin now." Though he felt unsettled by the incident, it quickly became submerged in the welter of strange and fascinating sensations that assailed him everywhere he turned in what he called the "colorful carnival which is India." But within days another series of events occurred which again brought into question the Center's practices and ideas. These events we will call, collectively, the *tambura incident.*

As I have noted, each morning after pre-dawn meditation, and after tea and breakfast, the students spent a couple of hours being instructed in sacred music by two professional musicians, Banduhl and Gajvadan by name.

They were old friends, or seemed to be, yet could not have been more different in style and temperament. Banduhl was thickly built, grounded, and still. His manner was quiet and calm, his intelligence of a pervading, enfolding kind. His complexion was even and smooth, his pleasantly rounded head completely bald across the top. He wore soft-toned blouses of banded colors, embroidered with patterns that conveyed the sense of stately, elegant reverence which he seemed to feel for all the world.

Gajvadan was of a different stripe. Short, wiry, and angular, his graying hair flowed loose, long, and free. He was electric. His stride was quick and jagged, driven by the sudden impulses which seemed to motivate him. His overlapping garments, in shades of unbleached linen and gray, hung away from his body willy-nilly, flapping wildly about like the gestures he made with bony hands that sparkled with large silver rings.

With the meditation students posed around the edge of a guest room at the Darshan Suites hotel, their backs to the wall, one of the musicians would sit on the bed that took up most of the floor, musical instruments arrayed before him. From this softly commanding position, these sons of Orpheus managed to convey the rudiments of several Sanskrit ragas over the course of their time with Robert and Gretchen's group of pilgrims.

Gajvadan and Banduhl frequently accompanied the group with the *tambura*, the stringed instrument which forms the foundation of much Indian classical music. The instrument's hypnotic pulsation is typically employed as a drone against which another instrument, or the human voice, articulates a melody. The strings are not manipulated with the weaker hand, like those of a guitar or viola, but are plucked in their open positions in a constant, unvarying rhythm, at a measured, steady pace. (Robert has insisted, quite excitedly, that I listen to several recordings on which the instrument can be heard.)

The guru and his assistant invested the tambura with distinctly spiritual properties. The twangy, pulsating quality of the sound it produced was claimed to act upon the Chakra system in much the same manner as the mantras the guru chanted in his hoarse, impassioned, and occasionally nasal, tones. As such, the tambura was thought of as not merely a musical instrument, destined for simple entertainment, but as a potent weapon in the arsenal of implements the guru deployed to unlock the vast but thwarted psychic potentials of his students.

Robert understood the pride of place enjoyed by the tambura in the guru's system and enthusiastically discussed the instrument, loading it with symbolic as well as practical meaning. The steady, unwavering manner in which the strings are plucked suggested to him the ideal of constant, regular effort at yogic practices considered necessary to bring the seeker to his goal. Oscillations created as the diminishing vibrations of one plucked string cross-faded into the expanding vibrations of its successors produced a series of troughs and crests, a pattern of overlapping waves which evoked the phenomenon of either light or of an ocean, both images pregnant in spiritual metaphor. Then there was the peculiar ability of the tambura to produce overtones—a series of secondary pitches growing out of the originally plucked note. Like ripples around a pond-thrown stone, like exponential numbers, a hall of mirrors, or the endless series of images produced by pointing a video camera at a television screen: criss-crossing in their subtle dance across a sea of sound, these ethereal tones suggested to Robert the infinity of both inner and outer space. Listening to the steady twanging of the tambura's strings, he felt his entire system, psychic as well as physical, syncing up to the most fundamental rhythms of the universe, while its ever-expanding overtones pulled him towards his highest aspirations . . .

Freighted as it was with such exalted implications, the tambura was surrounded by layers of protocol approaching those governing relations with the swami or the guru. It must be handled reverently and carefully. It must not be used merely for musical entertainment; instead it must remain pure in its role as sacred instrument, a life-giving and soul-releasing benefactor. Finally, it must be played only by those who are "ready"—those, that is, who have reached a certain level of "spiritual evolution." To allow someone insufficiently prepared to play the tambura would be akin to giving children the eucharistic chalice to make mud pies with. Several of the guru's students had asked, over the years, if they could acquire a tambura to employ in their daily mantra chanting, but the answer had invariably been, "No, you're not ready." To act against this advice would be to court the displeasure of the guru or his assistant and its inevitable corollary, "bad karma."

Given these considerations, the meditation students were startled one morning when, after conducting a particularly exuberant singing session, Banduhl innocently recommended that his protégés familiarize themselves more intimately with the hallowed instrument. As Banduhl's knowledge of English was rudimentary, he conveyed his wishes as much with gestures as with the disconnected words and phrases, extracted from the depths of memory, and after much effort, which constituted his practice of the language of his students. Extending the instrument on the bed in front of him, outstretched arms encompassing its length, he offered it up.

"You . . . come . . ." he began; and then, at a loss for words, he pantomimed plucking the tambura's strings in the careful, steady manner which the students were accustomed to observing. Neither the guru nor his assistant were present, as it was not their custom to attend the music lessons (where they were, no one knew exactly, though it was assumed they were at the swami's kutiya, since they were always there when the students arrived in their auto rickshaws, looking as if they had enjoyed an extensive visit). The guru's sister, Anjali, was there, however, and the students looked to her as a group, as she always joined enthusiastically in deciphering Banduhl's comments (the students would sit expectantly, encouraging smiles on their faces, offering possible translations of Banduhl's truncated phrases; Anjali listened attentively, sitting erect with the same earnest effort with which she joined in the singing lessons; finally she would interpose a question or two in some Indian language, apparently not Banduhl's own, for this seldom proved any more fruitful of an exact understanding than the students' probings in English; further probings and pantomimings would result, nonetheless, in communication sufficient for the occasion, at which a broad, sweet, smile would spread over Banduhl's face like a rising sun; with a small gesture of the shoulders he would then address himself once again to his instrument, take up the strain he had interrupted to correct the students, or to add a further elaboration to the scale or raga they had been practicing.)

In the case we are discussing, the students redoubled their efforts to make certain that they had understood Banduhl correctly, as the seeming import of his communication ran counter to their expectations.

"Come . . . here . . ." he repeated, indicating the room in which they sat, a room they were accustomed to enter only for their daily music lessons.

"You . . . practice" he continued, and he again proffered the tambura toward the students.

Robert caught Gretchen's eyes across the room. They conveyed surprise at Banduhl's suggestion, along with an obvious delight at the prospect of learning to play the tambura; after all, she had often gushed to Robert about its beautiful sonic properties, even emitting the "Ach!" (as in "Ach so schön!," another quirk she had picked up from her German mother) which she reserved for such epiphanic experiences as Brahms's *Second Symphony*, Rachmaninoff's famous piano concerto, or a particularly gorgeous sunset. Nor was Robert unmoved by Banduhl's offer to handle the beautifully fashioned instrument, its gourd-like body glowing with the soft luster of years of use. He didn't doubt that he would have little difficulty mastering the steady plucking of its strings, a feat which struck my friend, who was quite a decent guitarist, as completely elementary.

Anjali cleared things up with a final round of soundings, and after several quick nods to Banduhl she turned her attention to the students.

"He says that you should all come here and practice

playing the tambura," she said. "That way you can take turns accompanying the class during our music lessons."

Banduhl smiled and nodded around the room while Anjali spoke, placing his imprimatur on her translation.

Anjali further clarified that the instrument would be left in the music room, and that the door would be left unlocked. The students were invited to come at any time, day or night, and familiarize themselves with plucking the instrument's strings in the regular, steady manner required to support the sacred ragas and hymns in which Banduhl and Gajvadan were instructing them.

That afternoon Robert and Gretchen again relaxed in Gretchen's room, waiting for the time of darshan, when the phone rang. When Robert picked up he encountered the Enforcer's voice, a voice that was, on this occasion, strident, unpleasant, and to the point.

"What did Banduhl say about the tambura?"

Her tone, in Robert's phrase, was that of a policeman in hot pursuit of a band of thieves who, having collared one of them, demands, "Where are the others?"

Robert remained calm. He was put off by Johanna's tone, but it was one he had heard on a couple of other occasions. It was the tone that the Enforcer reserved for instances in which the customary systems of spiritual protocol—which Robert himself respected as a nexus of reverential displays toward persons, objects, and situations considered sacred— or even worse, the interests of the guru and his meditation center, were under threat.

"He said that we should come to the music room and practice the tambura," Robert replied, "so that we can take turns playing it during music lessons."

"He couldn't have said that," she shot back icily.

"We were all quite certain, even Anjali . . ."

"You must have misunderstood," the Enforcer interrupted bluntly, and then she hung up without ceremony.

Johanna's final remark—"You must have misunderstood"—burned into Robert's brain like a corrosive, cleansing acid. He knew what it meant to be gaslighted, and though he didn't think of Hitchcock's famous film at the time, he was feeling something like Ingrid Bergman. He and eight other responsible adults had witnessed Banduhl's invitation in the music room, and while translation was always difficult, the group had taken elaborate pains to make sure that there had been no misunderstanding.

He complained to Gretchen, in terms he repeated to me.

"It's not like she said, 'Perhaps you misunderstood . . .' or 'Are you sure you got it right?' No, she made a categorical statement, 'You *must* have misunderstood.'"

"Well . . ." was Gretchen's only reply.

"She couldn't really defend the Enforcer," Robert told me. "She was as certain as I about what Banduhl had said. But she wouldn't say anything against her. Gretchen thinks of Johanna like a revered parent, or some benevolent big sister, willing to take the trouble to point out all the bad habits which block your path toward self-mastery. If you think her mannerisms a little harsh, it's suggested that you haven't gotten over the harshness of your own mother! Finally you are reminded that the yogic path isn't one for sissies, and that if you can't stomach the truth, shorn of all the niceties that ensure that we never get each other's honest opinions, you can go back to eating MacDonald's and watching cable television."

"There's probably some reason . . ." Gretchen offered.

"I can't imagine what . . ." and his voice trailed off.

Robert recalled to me his first impression of the woman, at a special workshop in the Washington suburbs, whom he now called the Enforcer. She wore a different look then, and spoke with a different voice: a soft, musical voice inflected with the accent of the European country in which she was born and raised. Dressed in white kurta pajamas, she smiled openly when she extended her hand to meet Robert's. He had told Gretchen that she reminded him of Oz's Glinda, the Good Witch of the North, with her lilting voice and the aura of fairy godmother that seemed to surround her. Gretchen responded noncommittally, for reasons Robert now understood. He had seen only one face of the guru's assistant. Yet Gretchen knew, through years of association, that it was not the only one.

Nothing further was said about the tambura until the next morning's meditation session on the hotel's roof. After the chanting and the silent sitting; after the small bell was sounded to signal that eyes could be opened, that the lotus postures into which the students had torturously wrenched themselves could be relaxed, Johanna matter-of-factly stated that Banduhl's remarks were the result of a misunderstanding, and that under no circumstances were the students to make their way unattended to the music room, or to handle the tambura in any manner, on any occasion.

She then briefly rehashed the guru's ideas concerning the instrument and explained that, while Banduhl and Gajvadan were superb preceptors of Indian sacred music, they could not be expected to be familiar with the guru's rigorous system of self-development, and should not be regarded as exemplars in that sphere.

I will leave it to the reader to decide whether it was a mark of pettiness that Robert, over the next couple of days, took note of the fact that the Enforcer made no effort to apologize for cursorily dismissing his testimony regarding the tambura incident. Her manner on the phone had suggested to Robert that she thought him a dolt, with the reliability of a child.

"You must have misunderstood," she said emphatically, leaving no room for negotiation. Yet he took her remarks on the hotel roof as tacit admission that he, along with the rest of the students, had understood Banduhl perfectly well.

What troubled Robert more deeply—leaving aside the Enforcer's shrewish unpleasantness when she got into one of these snits—was that Johanna's remarks suggested that if Robert were to follow the guru's system, he must be willing to admit that his clear and certain perceptions about reality were not to be trusted, at least not if they were gainsaid by either the guru or the Enforcer. "While on the ontological level I found the proposition interesting," he told me, "I couldn't see accepting it on the operational."

The tensions created by the prasad and tambura incidents found relief only one day after the latter episode, when the daily routine of meditations, music lessons, and visits to the swami's hut was interrupted for a field trip into the Indian countryside. It was a Hindu holy day, and the guru had decided that a tour of several revered temples found in the locality, each hallowed by centuries of devotion, would be propitious. On this occasion the guru himself accompanied his students in the same small bus which had ferried them to Mysore from Bangalore.

They motored deep into the South India countryside, past endless fields where peasants in loin cloths worked under a broiling sun. In honor of the holiday, the group was under injunction to fast until midnight, an austerity that nevertheless permitted a few pieces of fruit bought at roadside stands along the way. The bus covered a great deal of ground during the day, though Robert had no precise idea where they had been; he was without a map, and no information was provided by the guru as to their whereabouts (the Enforcer had enjoined against bothering GuruJi with mundane questions during the tour: "he's your spiritual guide, not your tour guide"). But his lack of spatial orientation in no way diminished, and more likely enhanced, the impression the outing made on Robert, an impression of ancient life embedded in an ancient earth, and time without end. "You should've seen it," he enthused. "Men were tilling the fields with wooden plows, as their ancestors have done for thousands of years! Every now and then the bus would cross a bridge over a stream, and a peasant would be in the water with his buffalo, washing him down like some American blade with his new car!" Robert was much taken with the ancient temples the group visited, with their worn stone, elaborate carvings, and scampering monkeys. At one such stop he was even seized by an overwhelming sensation that he had walked those precincts in some forgotten past, a subjective experience about which I am at a loss to comment. Gretchen had come down with a cold that was running through the group, vindicating, for Robert, his hypothesis of ill health as the likely explanation for her stumble at the swami's kutiya. She had decided to forego the tour and rest at the hotel, hoping to recover before the next day's darshan with the swami.

The day was well advanced when the little bus returned to the Darshan Suites. The group ambled into the hotel, weary with the dust and sweat of South India, and still feeling the press of bodies they had encountered inside the temples. To keep their minds off their stomachs for the remainder of the day, the guru had arranged for the bus to transport them, after a brief rest, to the famous Brindavan pleasure gardens, which were not far away. He would not accompany them on this excursion, it having no sacred function; as for the Enforcer, she had been strangely absent since morning meditation. The students would instead be in Anjali's capable hands. The music teachers Banduhl and Gajvadan also stepped up into the bus before it pulled away.

It took the better part of an hour to reach the pleasure gardens. The group was quiet during the ride out except for Linda, who seldom stopped talking (though even her voice was subdued) and Anjali, an effusive and curious sort who periodically interjected observations on the passing scenery, or questioned the driver in a language her charges could not understand. As the bus approached Brindavan, a wide lake came into view on one side, while on the other the dry, rolling plains that had accompanied the pilgrims for the better part of their drive stretched to the distant horizon. After motoring along the lake for some time the bus pulled into a parking lot. Anjali took care of the group's admission fees at a small wooden booth. It stood at one end of a broad walkway which crossed the dam that held back that end of the lake.

"The air was charged as if with silver particles" when

this group—the western meditation students along with the two professional musicians and Anjali—slowly proceeded across the top of the dam. Anjali was more or less in front, though she frequently turned to comment to those behind her. The group spontaneously slowed their pace at the middle of the dam, where they stopped to take in the extraordinary scene. The lake, vast and broad, stretched out placidly to their left. A brushstroke of green hills could be made out on the far horizon, and over it all hung what Robert called a "sky of low clouds" in a poem he showed me. The day was waning. The sun was still above the horizon, but the light subdued with a sense of enormous energy barely contained; steel gray thunderheads appeared in the distance. There was, overall, a brooding quality to the moment, and one of impending revelation. Robert felt his inner core being drawn inexplicably toward the threshold of something he was inclined to speak of as "the infinite."

To the right of the group lay the dam's spillway. A gushing sheet of water, powerfully nudged by the enormous weight of the lake's mass, cascaded down its face. Robert recalled the musician Gajvadan's especial fascination with this spectacle: how he stood against the rail for some time peering into the thundering torrent, turning occasionally to speak with Banduhl, who took only infrequent, casual glimpses into the spillway. Gajvadan was smoking, as was his frequent custom, and when he waved the glowing, fuming wand through the charged air, it seemed to threaten some alchemical combustion to be followed, with utter certainty, by a general conflagration. Banduhl spoke in muted tones, his face composed. His eyes seemed to seek something within, while nonetheless taking in the extraordinary tableau which surrounded him.

Eventually the group continued over the causeway to the pleasure gardens, which occupied a large area of sloping ground past the watercourse into which the spillway dumped its torrent. The earth was terraced, and a series of steps led the visitors through successive stages of descending terrain. There were marble pavilions, ornamental walls, pools and fountains, and a cornucopia of flowering trees and bushes. Anjali led the group, more or less, enthusing over bright blossoms and wondering aloud about the names of the various shrubs and flowers.

On the way back over the causeway Gajvadan paused to again gaze into the spillway. Casting a final, cursory glance as he fell back in with the crowd leaving the gardens, he waved his cigarette dismissively toward the sky over the lake, that sky both serene and vaguely threatening . . .

As the minibus rumbled across the undulating plains, a large orange sun hung suspended on the horizon. Robert sat near the back, quietly watching the parched, scrub-covered land flow by. On the crest of a rise, the bus pulled over to allow a couple of the students to relieve themselves in the surrounding fields.

It was here, on a swell of high ground overlooking the surrounding plains, with the powerfully glowing ember of a setting sun about to pull down the shades on a holy day in India, that Robert underwent what he considers the culminating experience of his "journey to the source."

The scene was quiet, the road deserted. The occupants of the bus were tired from a long day of temple touring and wandering in the pleasure gardens. Jenni and one of the sisters had disappeared behind separate clumps of brush, discharging their biological needs. Robert sat next to an open window with no one beside him. Across the aisle, a few rows forward, Gajvadan and Banduhl conversed in muted tones. Ahead of them were Ward and Linda. Ward looked out the window toward the setting sun, vaguely listening to Linda, whose voice reached Robert only as the faintest murmur. Anjali had stepped down from the bus to await the return of the students who had gone to the bushes, attentive as ever to the simple, practical needs of her charges.

It was what cinematographers call the magic hour, that time at dusk when the diffuse light permeates everything with an uncanny beauty. A hush had descended over the plains, and Robert felt more alone than he had ever been. Gretchen was at the hotel, suffering with her cold. Neither the guru nor his assistant were present, and though Robert had come to question the former's system and the latter's sanity, they had provided some semblance of continuity with his past. He had only just become acquainted with his fellow pilgrims in India, and they were in any case absorbed in their accustomed, private worlds. Ward listened patiently to Linda; one of the sisters sat stilly, contentedly flushed but exhausted; the other was out among the bushes with Jenni. Heinz sat alone behind the driver, as serious and self-absorbed as ever. Anjali stood at the doorway of the bus like a sentry, or some protective deity, sharing an occasional remark with the driver.

Robert did not reflect, though it occurred to me immediately, when I first heard his story, that he was many thousands of miles from the place he was accustomed to call home. Nor did he possess, for that matter, any very precise idea about where he was. Had he been released on those plains he would not have known how to orient himself towards any familiar setting, be it the Darshan Suites hotel or his apartment in Washington, two oceans and several continents away. But if he did not reflect on these matters at the time, it was almost certainly due to the fact that, although he felt a solitude starker than he had ever known, he did not feel the sufferings of loneliness. Instead, with a deep sense of contentment, he felt himself sinking into a seamless communion with the world in which he was enfolded.

He recalled the guru's instruction of two days standing, conveyed after morning meditation at the Enforcer's daily briefing, to focus more on *sound* as they went through the rounds of their daily activities. This instruction was part and parcel of the guru's belief that modern society, along with the general run of humankind in any era, is excessively oriented toward the visual. The guru taught that an unhealthy fascination with the organ of sight, at the expense of the other senses, reflects an unfortunate focus on the ego (or, in terms of the traditional yogic belief structure which was always the guru's point of reference, a concentration of energy in the third Chakra, the ego's base). The guru charged this imbalance not only with the grasping and greed that permeate our lives, but also with the hollow sense of separateness that afflicts so many of us, the *anomie* first identified by the great sociologist Émile Durkheim over one hundred years ago.

The antidote to this grave disorder, and the heart of the guru's practices, was to develop the sense of hearing. Thus his focus on the chanting of mantra as the core of daily meditation practice, as well as the extreme delicacy surrounding the use of the tambura. Hearing, the guru taught, was connected with the fourth, or heart, Chakra, and as such with feeling and emotion. While an unbalanced ego Chakra isolates us in an illusion of a separate and distinct identity, the heart Chakra, when functioning properly, connects us with everything around us through feelings of love, compassion, and affinity.

Robert had practiced focusing on sounds over the two days since the guru's directive, particularly when he walked in the countryside after morning meditations. He discovered that he could notice many more aural stimuli than he was accustomed to perceiving, simply by listening. Though he enjoyed the experience, and found it fascinating, he had allowed his efforts to lapse on the day of the temple tour. There were many things to see that day, and many that were new and affecting, like the timeless fields, an open air cattle market, or the temple whose precincts he felt certain that he had wandered before. But as the crepuscular hush descended like a weight on the small bus, a solitary outpost of humanity on the isolated plain, the guru's instructions again came upon him like a soft wind from within.

He gazed out the open window over the dusk-muted gold of the rolling landscape. He felt pleasantly fatigued from the day's efforts, and the fast he had followed with the rest of the group rendered his senses particularly acute. He allowed himself to become aware of the myriad sounds that made up the aural fabric of his surroundings. The driver had cut the engine to conserve fuel and, as the road was completely deserted, and this section of the countryside devoid of human constructions, there remained no sounds but those produced by nature and its creatures.

There was, within the bus, the low murmur of the musicians' soft voices; and fainter still, an occasional remark by Linda who, in her exhaustion, had become unusually reticent. From beyond the bus Robert first noticed a soughing sound. This was the light breeze which played across the low bushes that covered the earth on those plains.

Closing his eyes so that he might give himself wholly over to listening, Robert attempted to identify an undifferentiated buzzing which he now perceived to be mingled with the breeze; as he focused his attention here, he realized that the buzzing consisted of innumerable insects producing their varying sounds at once. He screwed his concentration down another notch and, after a moment, the perception of undifferentiated buzzing gave way to an absurd awareness of each of the many separate insect calls of which the greater hum was composed. These sounds varied strikingly in pitch, quality, and intensity, as well as in the duration and rhythm of their unique patterns. There must have been thousands, if not millions,[4] of insects in the surrounding plains. Robert, astonished, suddenly realized that he was aware of each and every one of them.

After dwelling for some time in the sensation of individual sounds, an operation which brought Robert a sensation akin to spiritual joy, he inwardly felt himself take another plunge towards the heart of these emanations. He now again perceived the blending together of the myriad individual buzzings, clickings, chirpings, and rubbings, but this time without ceasing to distinguish their separate

---

4 According to Larry Pedigo and Marlin Rice, there are 400 million insects in the average acre of land. *Entomology and Pest Management*, 2008.

natures. He noted a general undulation, a rising and falling of the insect soundwave, with common pauses, crescendos and decrescendos. It was as if those innumerable minuscule creatures were acting in concert, like some massive symphony cut loose from the moorings of its conductor, following an inner direction which just happened to produce a result of exquisite, organized beauty!

My friend reports that he soon found himself abruptly caught up in a vibrant pulsation, one which took in not only the vast insect symphony but also the soughing of the breeze, the faint murmurs of conversation in the bus, the orange sun dropping into the far horizon, and the steady throbbing of blood through his veins. Eyes closed, oblivious to all else, he was now completely absorbed in a universe of sound. His psyche synced now with distinct troughs and crests, waves which advanced and receded, overtaking one another, cross-fading and blending in beautiful circular repetitions. The most delicate of the sounds—the smallest of the insects, I imagine—formed the froth on this ocean, building one upon the other, their varying pitches answering their predecessors in a series of harmonic vibrations . . .

"And there it was!" Robert erupted as he recounted the experience. "It struck me between the eyes, like a bolt from a crossbow. The entire universe had become one massive tambura, and I was dead in the middle of it!" Sitting on that bus, permeated with those sounds, a sense of profound peace suffused my friend from the inside out. Surprisingly, or perhaps not, the "tambura incident" did not cross his mind. He was instead, for that moment at least, filled with affection for the entire universe and grateful to Gretchen, who had encouraged him to make the "journey," for having brought him to this extraordinary juncture.

He was jolted by the sound of the engine kicking over; in moments the bus resumed its rumbling over the rough road back to Mysore. The sun had disappeared over the horizon, and it was growing dark.

The "Journey to the Source" was nearing its end, and two days later Robert and Gretchen, along with the remainder of the guru's group, traveled back to Mumbai to await their flights to the United States. As the students had time to kill in that sprawling and unearthly city ("partaking of heaven or hell, I wasn't sure which") it was recommended by the guru that they visit the Elephanta Caves. There occurred the last of those experiences to which Robert has attached a transcendent significance. In the mind of my friend, in fact, this incident came to serve as a punctuation mark upon the entire journey, affirmation that everything which had transpired in India, both pleasant and unpleasant, had happened for a good and vital purpose.

I refer to this episode as the *breathing statue incident*.

The Elephanta Caves, located on an island close off the shore at Mumbai, are considered by art historians to be one of the most magnificent examples of rock-hewn architecture ever created. Into the island's solid basalt hillsides, a sixth century Hindu king commanded the construction of colonnaded chambers filled with colossal relief sculptures dedicated to the god Shiva. In a rare moment of camaraderie, the guru himself accompanied Robert and Gretchen, as well as Ward and Linda—the only other students who chose to make the trip—to Mumbai's harbor, where he left them to pursue his own mysterious affairs. At the Gateway of

India's stolid arch the four westerners caught the chugging ferry toward Elephanta Island.

Ward was the only male in the group besides Robert and Heinz (the older, sour, and reclusive Dutchman) and Robert and he had spent numerous hours walking into the countryside after morning meditations, past a marsh and down a shaded dirt lane that debouched on a larger road near a horse-racing track. Ward, who had become involved with the guru, he explained to Robert, after undergoing a prison sentence on cocaine charges, credited the older man with helping him to put his life in order. He was now married and happy and working in the family business. More important, he was free of his former addiction. He possessed an unassuming manner, and a natural sweetness, and it was clear that Robert, from the way he spoke of the man, enjoyed his company.

The pilgrims took places on the ferry's bow where, sitting back against the pilot house, they felt the sea breeze wash across them. When the boat docked at the base of the hump of green that constituted the island on the slopes of which the caves were located, they clambered onto the wooden pier and walked toward the lush mountainside that rose before them. There was a well-kept path lined with the tables of peddlers of devotional trinkets, and also displays of purely secular art and craft objects. Since Ward and Linda wanted to linger over the tables, Gretchen and Robert proceeded up the mountainside on their own, accompanied by the vocalizations of monkeys that scampered through the trees and across the path.

The high-ceilinged caves were dark and damp; into their broad, deep niches were carved the monumental sacred images. Gretchen caught her breath at the sight of each splendid sculpture, the object of centuries of the kind of religious devotion she had learned to apply to the small replicas that sat on her private altar at home. Robert was particularly struck by the colossal joined heads of Brahma, Vishnu and Shiva Maheshvara: a Hindu trinity of sorts: creator, preserver, and destroyer.

Before leaving the caves, Gretchen and Robert stood before a sculpted image of the god Shiva in seated meditation. The god's face, with eyes softly closed, expressed a sublime peace. His hands lay in his lap, one upon the other, the palms up in an attitude of supreme acceptance. The legs were folded under him in a classic lotus position.

The statue was situated just inside the one of the cave's entrances, where the diffuse light created a soft sheen across the worn, dark stone. Whether as a result of this *effet de lumière;* or on account of the arduous walk up the mountainside; or the difficulty, upon emerging from the dark and damp of the cave's interior, of adjusting his eyes to the half-light near the cave's entrance; it was here that Robert underwent the last remarkable experience of his journey. Though I hesitate to relate something so outlandish, I have committed to telling my friend's story just as he told it to me, and so I will state the fact baldly. Robert has asserted, and without a trace of irony, that standing before the Shiva sculpture, just inside the entrance to one of the caves, he perceived the chest of the solid stone statue moving slowly in and out—as if it were breathing! (breathing deeply and evenly, according to Robert, as in meditation)!

"Gretchen," he whispered, "this is really strange."

"I know."

"What are you talking about?!"

"It seems to be . . . breathing," she answered, her voice hushed.

For what it's worth, Robert looks upon Gretchen's corroboration of his perceptions as, if not proof positive, then strong evidence that something supernatural occurred at the caves. He and Gretchen stood motionless for a long moment, hand in hand, before moving silently into the bright of the afternoon.

Having spent too much time in the temples, they had to sprint past the peddlers' tables to catch up to Ward and Linda, who gestured emphatically from the pier, where the ferry was preparing to depart. The guru would be waiting for them at the Gateway of India; it would be a grievous affront to miss an appointment with the "teacher." Gretchen and Robert scrambled on to the ferry, well winded, just as it was shoving off.

&&&

I feel compelled, as a close, to say a few words about Robert's story. After all, there is much that could be questioned, analyzed, and even outright refuted. If we accompany Robert on his excursion into the subjective—accepting at face value that he saw a statue breathing, or that the "entire universe" became "one vast tambura"—there is little left to say. If we take the opposite tack, and seek a psychological explanation (be it in the strangeness of the setting, expectations created by the guru, the effects of fasting or the force of Robert's own long-standing wish to feel "at one" with the universe) we reduce Robert to a hapless pawn of either external forces or internal weaknesses. Rightly or not, I have too much respect for the intelligence and, indeed, the sheer will power of my old friend to lightly accept either of these hypotheses.

Let me just say that Robert went to a distant and foreign land ("more like another planet than another country," he once remarked); that he spent time with a man said to be a "highly evolved being"; that he received this man's blessing in the form of *prasad* distributed after each daily *darshan*; that three golden eagles circled the sky upon the arrival of Robert and his companions at the holy man's dwelling; that he wore a woman's clothing for a day or two; that he was instructed in the singing of devotional music by two extraordinary men; that he visited ancient temples on a Hindu holy day, fasting as was the custom of the country; that he saw a land where time had stopped; that, led to a pleasure gardens, he stood atop a dam between a broad lake and a gushing torrent under a clear yet brooding sky, where Gajvadan's cigarette threatened to ignite the entire universe into a sudden ball of fire; that he found himself enmeshed in a world of uncannily subtle beauty while sitting in a bus stopped on a deserted road on a rise above the dry plains in the region of Mysore; and finally, that he witnessed a statue of Shiva breathing at the Elephanta Caves near Mumbai.

Naturally I question many of the guru's claims, as well as his methods. Leaving to one side that the concept of "highly evolved" beings, the existence of the Chakra system, or the reality of metempsychosis, though all long accepted in the East, are without any basis in modern science, the guru's methods raise an eyebrow or two. The draining fasts; the complicated protocols governing relations, not only with the swami, but with the guru himself and everything associated with him; the guru's inaccessibility; and the blatant good-cop, bad-cop routine which he and his assistant kept up: all of these things seemed designed to keep the students off balance. Objects promising the liberation his disciples so ardently sought—the swami, the tambura—were tantalizingly dangled in front of their noses, only so that they could be told that an impenetrable, spiritual *cordon sanitaire* blocked access to them.

At my most cynical I incline to view the guru's entire operation as nothing more than a clever money-making racket. After all, the "Journey to the Source" was not cheap. The "Darshan" Suites hotel; the villagers who lined the road to greet the swami's visitors; even the flock of sheep herded through the streets of the town—were these all part of some darshan assembly line, devised expressly to soak silly westerners with more money and spiritual longing than common sense? Did the swami really live in that cramped hut, or during the long hours of the guru's and his assistant's absence prior to darshan, while their disciples were fasting, contemplating the evils of ego, or solemnly entoning sacred ragas, were they and the swami enjoying a good lunch at a western hotel; or, for that matter, over at the racetrack, betting the student's hard-earned money on a promising three-year-old and having a broad laugh at their expense?

These are only some of the many questions which I am sure will never be answered. Robert has severed his ties with the guru's operation, which he implicates in the breakup of his marriage (a nasty business, I'm sure). Yet he keeps coming back to that bus, and he feels certain that something fundamental occurred there, something that changed his life irrevocably. The damnedest thing, and what keeps the whole blasted episode on my mind, is that as unwilling as I am to accept the legitimacy of the guru's system, I am unable to dismiss my friend's certainty about the importance of an experience which could not have taken place absent the framework of that system's practices and protocols. For wasn't it the guru who suggested that his students concentrate on sounds? And could Robert have possibly understood the full significance of this instruction had he not been guided for several years in the chanting of mantra? Wasn't it also the guru who encouraged him to go to India, who secured the services of the musicians whose daily singing lessons heightened his sensitivities and broadened his appreciation of the tambura? And was it not the guru who brought him to the swami, exposing him to an outlook that would ultimately render the guru's own services obsolete?

Even the "tambura incident," which originally struck me as nothing more than a bit of personal unpleasantness, seems to have played a vital role in setting up Robert's life-changing experience. Robert himself agrees that having the instrument, an alluring symbol of his spiritual aspirations, dangled in front of him by Banduhl, only to be withheld by Johanna, forced him to focus even more energy on the attainment of those goals. One would almost credit "the Enforcer" with orchestrating the entire scenario, sacrificing herself (acting the shrewish, menopausal bitch) in order to drive Robert toward some further revelation, without regard to her own popularity or reputation. But how could she have done so?

Was Banduhl also in on the scheme?

His halting English, just an act?

And how could Johanna have known that the bus would stop at dusk on the deserted plains, where unnumbered insects created a universal tambura, free for anyone who might listen, just at a moment when Robert was ready to recognize such an experience? It is hard to avoid the conclusion that something far more powerful, and far more knowing than the Enforcer—or for that matter, the guru or the swami—must have orchestrated these experiences. After all, which of these personalities could make the sun set like a giant orange ball, or make the water of the lake gush over the spillway under a brooding sky?

One last issue, and that is this. At the heart of the matter is Robert's sense of the importance of these events. If we dismiss his experience on the bus, or at the Elephanta Caves, as mere fantasy, then I have wasted your time and mine with a lot of poppycock. But there is that old respect for my friend's intelligence and, indeed, perspicacity. He does seem to have a better grip not only on who he is these days, but also on how he fits into the wider scheme of things—what he now likes to call the great, big, universal tambura. He has even made a nascent attempt to have some of his scribblings published.

Of course I wish him luck.

I gives me pleasure to think that talking about these experiences with me, an old, dear friend, has helped Robert to put some kind of cap on the entire affair. It will not be the final one, I'm sure, as these heart-swamping events reverberate across our lives like the overtones of my buddy's famous tambura.

By the way, if I have touched only lightly on the "statue incident," as compared to my treatment of the prasad and tambura incidents, it is because its significance can be summed up rather easily. Since it came on the last day of his stay in India, Robert (ever one to look for patterns, to create a story with a beginning, a middle, and an end) looks upon the episode as a conclusion of sorts. The statue, worn and dark, radiating serenity with its every feature—the softly closed eyes, hands lying placidly, palms up, on the crossed legs, timeless and immovable yet, yet (well, let's go ahead and say it!) breathing, breathing with the rhythm of a universe whose heart is ever still—seemed to say to Robert that after all the agitation of the trip, the cultural and geographic dislocations, the difficult and tiring travel, the strain of observing exotic customs and elaborate protocols, the changes he went through in his feelings about the guru and Johanna and even the personal enmities that raised their ugly heads, that the heart of things was still, and always will be, *peace*. Whether the statue really breathed, well, that's what he felt, and perhaps that's all that's important. But I am beginning to sound like Robert now ...

In any case, I've got to run. I promised an attractive graduate student we'd have lunch and talk about her program.

Om, and all that!

Another Friday Night (1982)

FRIDAY. There was a certain feel to it. Surely it was liberation from work, a liberation felt in smaller degree on other evenings of the week. You've come out to Virginia Avenue after a long day of typing waybills, with the traffic still heavy, a hushed excitement in the cooling air and a sense of expectancy. Friday meant knowing that you were finished; you had laid down your burden and Monday seemed forever away.

You were young.

You walk past the neat rows of townhouses all painted different colors. At the Foggy Bottom station you make your way through the milling throng that pours into the escalator like water down a drain. You reach 23rd Street and head for Pennsylvania Avenue.

Gary and Alan are waiting at Mr. Henry's. You'll sit at a sidewalk table and eat their tacos, something not quite Mexican, with lots of ground beef, and drink the house wine or draft beer. There will be a good flick at the Circle or down at the Biograph, a foreign film or some old classic. After the film you might make your way to the place above the college bar where the jazz is good for a three-dollar cover.

Another Friday Night (1982)

Most intriguing, to your young man's soul, Jen might come. She might come for dinner, or she may show up at the movies. She may even glide into the club sometime later. Jen's the kind of young woman, when you drop her off she presses a scrap into your hand, smiling the smile of a girl who has everything she needs. As she glides away you glance at the note, and it says *all that glitters isn't gold*; or *those who say don't know, and those who know don't say.*

You met her at Gretchen's house, Gretchen the Austrian who works with you at the exporting firm. You knew that Gretchen considered Jen family practically. She and Dirk had more or less adopted her, to the extent that anyone so, well, free, could be adopted—her own scant family having been lost to some backwash of personal history. You got on with Gretchen famously. The two of you shared an abiding interest in the poetry of Pablo Neruda and Argentinean tango. Gretchen and Dirk wouldn't have introduced just anyone to Jen, but Gretchen decided you were okay, and Dirk went along with her on such matters. So you were invited to the dinner party at the townhouse on Capitol Hill, and it was one of those times you felt like Balzac's Eugène de Rastignac. You had found a protectress, you were on your way . . .

Gary and Alan are on the terrace when you approach the café. Gary is gesturing emphatically. Alan just nodded.

"Look who's here," Gary said.

They were discussing capital punishment. Gary was for it.

"What do you think, Brad? Say it was your mother or sister, wouldn't you want the guy to fry?"

"I don't know," I said as I got myself seated, "can you

condemn killing, and then make an example of someone by killing them?"

"That's what I've been trying to say," Alan put in, leisurely sipping his beer.

"I don't know," Gary said, shaking his head and looking at an indefinite point down the avenue, "if someone did that to someone I love, I'd think I'd want to see 'em fry."

His tone was questioning, as if he were willing to consider our point of view. One thing about Gary—or Alan, for that matter—they never got bitter when you disagreed with them. I suppose that's why we could have these sorts of discussions and still remain friends.

A waiter showed up with the tacos and falafel sandwiches, and after settling into our plates, Gary changed the topic.

"So, Brad, have you figured out what you're going to do about law school?"

I had interrupted my law studies a year earlier. Since then, the issue of whether I would return to the university had hung over my life like a blue haze.

"I'm not sure," I said. "I'm just taking it as it comes."

Gary wasn't satisfied with that response. He had developed a healthier respect for the practical realities of life than I.

"How are things going at your job? What are the prospects there?"

"I don't know, after a couple of years processing waybills, it's conceivable I could move up in the firm."

The fact is, moving up in the firm didn't interest me. It's true that I frequently agonized over the lack of any forward motion in my career. Nor was I content living at my mother's apartment, not feeling established enough to set up house on my own. But at bottom, there was something that concerned me more, something hard to define but more real to me than anything.

"Pussy," Alan said when I tried to explain.

He was so happy with his quip he almost spit out his beer.

"Just kidding," he added, wiping his mouth with his napkin.

Gary and Alan were my friends from high school years. Since I'd returned from university we had been hanging our regularly, our venue of choice that section of town from Dupont Circle and its environs, down through Foggy Bottom and across M Street into Georgetown. Yes, the city, with its structures, its evenly laid out streets and grand avenues, its arthouse cinemas, its cafés and jazz bars, its traffic circles and fountains, this was our fascination. Gary was happy working promotions at a big record company. Alan was programming computers to support his enthusiasms—for cinema, for jazz, for dope. But there was something else in the city, something beyond even its outward forms, its manifest face which in itself we found so beguiling, some occult essence that I, in any case, could feel, could breath, could almost touch.

It was this that intrigued me more than anything, how to get to that inner core, to somehow be that very quality that drew you inexorably into the city and its processes, its endless festival.

Where did Jen come in? She was the wild card. Before her I thought I knew the city, what I was dealing with. It was a chamber music concert at the Phillips, a foreign flick with the boys, the slanting sun of late afternoon slicing through the fountain at Dupont Circle; it was more than anything the breath of excitement in the air when you stood on the heights of Connecticut Avenue and looked down its length at the cafés and restaurants, the book and record shops, the people on the sidewalks.

But with Jen—what was it?—it was more like the river, its murky waters enveloping Roosevelt Island as it pushed past the Kennedy Center and under the bridge towards the Chesapeake. Sometimes after work she would be waiting; the two of us would go down to the river, walk along the bank all the way to the circle where they plant the big red canna lilies.

On our first date I had stopped at the car and kissed her. We were on a street in Georgetown, under a tree whose low branches hung heavily with luxuriant foliage. She didn't mind the fact of the kiss, but I kissed too long and too hard, and she pushed me softly away.

I apologized after we pulled away from the curb.

"It's nothing."

"I just want to get next to you," I said. It was a phrase I had heard and thought she would like. Later I came to know that she had been out with many men, many of them older than me, and realized there wasn't much I could have done that would have shocked her. She knew the ways of men, the kinds of things they might do, especially with a pretty woman like her.

When we got to Gretchen's house, where she lived, we made out in the car.

I was in a constant state of agony over her. Like that first kiss, I never knew if I had gone too far or not far enough.

She was a sphinx, but without the question, only answers; it was up to you to know the questions. What's more, she wasn't troubled to settle your mind by volunteering anything that might put you on a clearer course. That was your problem, one I doubt she gave much thought to . . .

Sometimes I drank myself silly, or took a long walk through the park. But there were other times, like Friday evenings when I met Gary and Alan at Mr. Henry's, when there was an expansive quality to the late summer evening, and I felt so liberated from work and toil that I could take an easygoing attitude. I was under the spell of Cortázar's great novel *Hopscotch* in those days, and at times I felt the entire thing to be one big, glorious game, with *synchronicity* spinning the wheel, deciding who would move next. Maybe she would show up, maybe she wouldn't. None of it really mattered. I could always have a few more beers, until I ended up like the guy in the Jacques Brel song: "Je serais bien dans une heure, je serais sans espoir . . ."[1]

What did we know about one another, after all?

She was pretty, and Gretchen's friend. She was fascinated with the Carlos Castaneda books I loaned her. She also was looking for something beyond the raw facts of the city, something even more powerful than that!

When we walked by the river she didn't hold my hand, or drape an arm over my shoulder the way another girl might have done. That wasn't her way. We talked about art and psychology; but later she would give herself all at once and that was that.

What was I to her?

A friend?

---

1. "I will be well in an hour; I will be without hope."

Just another man?

We were both trying to achieve the critical velocity to break free from old patterns. I was still holed up at my mother's place, uncertain how I would live in the future. She was a desultory student posing for fashion ads on the side. She showed a talent for painting but didn't pursue it with any real purpose.

She would talk about moving to a higher energy level, like some kind of human electron.

"Energy feeds on itself," she liked to say.

She sometimes alluded to someone who had taught her important things about life. I wasn't so astute as to inquire who this mysterious figure might be. Perhaps I didn't want to know. The city grew larger. She didn't change what I knew of the city, merely superimposed another element on what had been there.

Gary and Alan and I walked down Pennsylvania Avenue and, in the waning light followed M Street to Georgetown. The Key Theatre was playing the flamenco ballet film, *Bodas de Sangre*. It was the first of Carlos Saura's films featuring Antonio Gades, the great Spanish dancer, a danced rendition of Lorca's desperate love triangle.

The boys were uncertain what to make of it.

"It could have used more dialogue," Gary pronounced quizzically, "don't you think?"

"I don't know," Alan said, "I could see what they were going for, in that artsy-shmartsy kind of way."

"It just seemed like the camera spent an awful lot of time on the dancers' faces," Gary rejoined, "or just moving around the room. I guess I would liked to have seen more plot."

Another Friday Night (1982)

For my part, I was spellbound. Gades' brave strokes, and the searing presence of prima ballerina Cristina Hoyos, not to mention the brilliant guitar work of Paco de Lucía and his colleagues, left me in a state of heightened awareness, a sort of altered consciousness.

"I thought it was great," I told the boys, "like nothing I've ever seen . . . that kind of condensed passion, all within the framework of that kind of precision, that kind of control!"

"I don't know," Gary said, "maybe you need a lay or something." Alan just smiled.

We had come out of the theatre. There was Jen on the opposite sidewalk, vaguely looking around, this way and that. She made quite a picture in her dark dancer's tight and long, cotton print skirt. She hadn't noticed us, and I didn't approach her right away; it was too fine to watch her against the backdrop of the lights on the avenue, the cars full of fevered young people looking for life.

She saw us and came over. We walked to the river and took a sightseeing boat from the pier at the bottom of the avenue. The boat chugged downstream past the bold angles of the Kennedy Center and, father on, floodlit monuments to national greatness. We guys sat at a table drinking beers. Jen held the rail with one hand while she traced fanciful, balletic movements with her other limbs.

"You've got yourself quite a beauty there," Gary said, watching her.

"She's a beauty all right, but I don't know that I've got her."

"What's the story?" he asked.

"I'm not sure. She's not the kind of girl you get a hold

on. If you grasp too hard, she sort of . . . evaporates."

"An old story," Alan put in.

It was an old story, but it was a new one for me.

Jen returned to the table. She didn't drink; she was moving toward that higher energy level. You could feel it, see it. Gary asked about her classes, about her modeling work. He had always been the kind to reach out to people.

She wanted to take more dance classes.

"With dance," she said, "I feel like you can let your body find its natural rhythms, and through that, take part in all the larger energies—even those at the very core of life."

"That sounds like a handful."

"I guess so," she said, "but I have some very wise teachers."

There she went again, alluding to those gurus.

"Besides," she added, "what else is there?"

I think Gary knew what else there was. There was a solid career, money in the bank, a home, marriage, kids, a sound retirement strategy. But he didn't respond to her question, other than to say, "I guess you have a point there."

Alan sat smiling, already looking forward, I knew, to the joint he would light up as soon as he got home.

When the boat docked Alan and Gary parted company with Jen and me. They moved off toward the lights of Georgetown, and we walked along the river. She seemed everything I could have wanted at that moment, everything a woman might be. When we stopped to look over the rail into the current, she continued the dance-like movements she had practiced on the boat. That energy was rising, rising to some place I couldn't conceive of. It was as if she wanted to ascend above the city, float above its mass, while

Another Friday Night (1982)

I wished to sink deeper into its life, its passions. I took her around the waist. We kissed. Her mouth was soft and moist; her breasts pressed pleasantly against my chest. Then she skipped off, my desires irrelevant.

I saw her home in a cab. I knew I wouldn't be able to come up; Gretchen and Dirk had two young children whose room was beside Jen's. I dropped her off and went home.

It was another Friday night.

www.ingramcontent.com/pod-product-compliance
Lightning Source LLC
Chambersburg PA
CBHW020616120726
47905CB00003B/814